THE ACCOLADE

THE ACCOLADE

J. J. HERON

iUniverse, Inc.
New York   Bloomington

iUniverse books may be ordered through booksellers or by contacting:

iUniverse
1663 Liberty Drive
Bloomington, IN 47403
www.iuniverse.com
1-800-Authors (1-800-288-4677)

Because of the dynamic nature of the Internet, any Web addresses or links contained in this book may have changed since publication and may no longer be valid. The views expressed in this work are solely those of the author and do not necessarily reflect the views of the publisher, and the publisher hereby disclaims any responsibility for them.

ISBN: 978-1-4401-7450-6 (sc)
ISBN: 978-1-4401-7448-3 (dj)
ISBN: 978-1-4401-7449-0 (ebook)

Library of Congress Control Number: 2009911371

Printed in the United States of America

iUniverse rev. date:11/03/09

MaryAnn Rita
To My Family
I hope you will forgive me!!

Prologue

Aristotle : "asserted that man is a political animal."

CHAPTER ONE

▼

In Sixteen 0 nine (1609) The Captain of the Royal Guard to King James I, was told to seek out information from Madam Luan wife of Archbishop Luan and go to the castle. The Captain known by all as a ladies man had other reasons for being there while the Archbishop was away. The Archbishop was trying to get rid of King James the First. Working to get information about the Archbishops plans The Captain had one of his biggest men take care of Madam Luan and some of his other men took care of the Madam's servants. Captain Tyne's headman Thomas found all the information, and turned it over to Captain Tyne. Reporting to the King, Captain Tyne gave the information to the King. After reading all of it, he smiled, now he had to be careful about what to do with the Archbishop. He called Captain Tyne to his chambers to have a secret meeting and to give the Captain his orders to be carried out and to make sure no one knows about it. By chance, the Archbishop never returned to that part of England and was never heard form again. There for all his Land and belongings was taken over by King James the First. For his reward, The King James gave Captain Tyne his choice of any land in the kingdom and was made a Duke. The new Duke chose land in the north of England. There the Duke established his place in history. The Duke built a castle on the side of a mountain that over looked the whole of his estate. There after he and his ancestors that followed where known as The Dukes of Tyne. The first Duke Took care of his troops and the people who live on his estate. And they took care of the land and the Dukes that followed. In each generation, nothing changed to any big degree.

The Sixth Duke of Tyne
1877 to 1953

The Sixth Duke of Tyne Was my Grandfather Thomas Eaton Heron. His Wife was the Duchess of Tyne Ellen Williams Heron. They had four children:

The first-born was a son, the next inline to become The Duke of Tyne; Wilfred Mirgatroy Heron, he was married to Irene Helen Heron.

Their Children were: Joseph Paul the oldest and the second in line for the Title following his Father Wilfred and the youngest was Thomas William *(Me)* Third inline for the title of Duke of Tyne.

The second child was Reginald Thomas Heron he was married to Ann Olympia they had no children.

The third child was Margret Elizabeth she was married to John Stewart.

No living children.

The fourth child was William Haven he was married to Florence Mischuck.

Three children (a step-son) Jack and their two children William and Florence

The oldest grandson my brother Joseph Paul was born July 5 1928

I was born on March 9th 1929.That was my Grandfather's Birthday too.

As the Second World War was smoldering in Europe the Duke call my father to his library and discussed the future of the Dukes estate.

The Duke said "Wilfred I want you to make a home in the United States of America. At least you will be safe. I have investments in America and you will have to manage the business, which is in New York City, but you will have to live in The State of Connecticut, Where I own a large office building and some homes. Both are near New York City, where the main Office is located. You will need your brothers to help you, you will have to talk to them about going with you I have one more request. I want you to leave your son Thomas William here with the Duchess and me. That would make her extremely happy.

If you say yes, .You will have to go as soon as possible. Let me know after you talk to your wife and your brothers. I will arrange for all of you to on the HMS Queen Mary, from London. I am going to be in London next week it is important that you act fast. I will talk to Thomas William after you go now."

My father nodded, feeling the excitement of going back to America again. He was there before with the Duke and Duchess.

"Here's what I want you to do," The Duke went on. "These days it's difficult to run a business from England. It was never easy, but now it is hard because of the lack of communications. Go now, call your two brothers and your sister together, and ask them who want to stay in England and who want to go to the Unite States. I would do this myself but I do not want to influence them in any way, it will have to be their own choice. Call Thomas William and send him to me and the Duchess."

As my father left the library, he could not keep his excitement level down to normal. He ran all the way to his apartment. To tell my mother. My father wanted to know if my mother wanted to go to America, She was surprised at first. Father told her what the Duke said about living in the United States. His brothers will be asked to come too. His sister Margaret Elizabeth has a choice to come or stay here. Mother asked about the children. Father said the duke wanted Joseph Paul to go that we will be safe to carry on the Dukedom in England. , that the Duke wanted to keep Thomas William with him and the duchess. Mother was not too happy about that, she said, "if Thomas William wants to stay I will have no objections. In addition, I would love to go. I will tell Joseph Paul to start packing.

When my father found me in the stables, he said, "Your Grandfather wants to see you in the library as soon as possible wash your face and hands and go."

I was surprised and curious as to what was important that I had to see him fast. I did what my father asked me to do. I walked over to the horse's trough and washed in cold water, and went to see what was important. As I entered the Dukes Library I saw the Duke and Duchess, the Duke was sitting near his large mahogany desk in a brown leather chair. I knew something big was going to happen he never sat there. I turned and looked at the Duchess who looked worried about what was to come. Grandma gave me a small smile and patted the cushion next to her indicating for me to sit next to her. As I walked over to the Duchess, she put out her beautiful soft right hand to me. I grabbed it with both of my hands and sat next to her. I loved these two people much. I looked up at Grandma and smiled knowing I would always be safe with them.

The Duke sitting in his chair a cross from Grandma and me said

"Thomas William we have something to ask you and the answer you give us will not stop us from loving you. After you answer, I will tell you all about what is going to happen.

The Big Change

The Duke said" This is a bad time for all of us in England because of the war. I will need you to stay on the estate and care for The Duchess while I am away. I have asked your Father to go to The United States and run my businesses along with your mother and brother, and your two uncles. They will be gone for a long time, until the war is over; no one knows when that will be. Your father is going to give me their answer soon. The Duchess and I wanted you to know first so you will not be surprised or left out of what is to take place soon. Do you under stand what we are asking you to do."

I looked at Grandma than Grandfather and cried "Yes! Yes! I Love you both much I want to stay here. "

The Duchess hugged me and cried and the Duke got out of his chair came over to me picked me up from Grandmas arms and gave me a big hug and a kiss. Grandma got up and the three of us hugged The Duchess and I cried we were happy.

When my Father came back to see The Duke he had a big smile and looked happy. He told the Duke what took place in the first floor Library when everyone showed up. Father told them what the Duke had said. My father asked if had any questions before they gave my father their answer.

My father's sister Margaret Elizabeth Asked "am I included in going to The United States. "

My father said "yes."

Margaret Elizabeth said, "Good than I'm going, maybe I'll find me a rich Texan

Uncle Reggie Said " I have nothing to keep me here maybe I'll find a rich widow and let her keep me in the style I've become accustom to". They all laughed.

William Haven the youngest laughed and said, "If you all think you're going to me here your crazy.

That made it unanimous

My Father said, "I'll inform the Duke to make the arrangements for all of us.

If you have any questions from now on, go and ask the Duke.

Everyone was surprised that I wasn't unset about staying in the castle with The Duke and Duchess. But I was the happiest kid in all of England. This made The Duke And Duchess happy and sad, Sad because their children that were born here at the castle and raised in England were leaving their home and will be missed by them. And happy, I'll be staying with them. You would think that I would be sad to see them all go, but at the age of innocence I didn't know any better I loved the thought of having the Duke and Duchess all to my self. I was taking care of by both of them, and the castle staff.

As the war got hotter. The Germans started to bomb the larger cities in the south of England, London, Portsmouth, Plymouth, and Bristol. The Duke was called by his boyhood friend and classmate Winston Churchill, to come to London for a secret meeting.

Winston said, "Do not tell a soul about it, not even the castle staff." He told everyone including the Duchess and me," I'm going to Salisbury to do some important business and buy some things that are need at the castle and I will be gone for two days, "

I cried, when are you coming back , Grandfather laughed and said, " In two days and I want you to take care of The Duchess and be mindful of the Staff while I'm gone you can do that.

I looked at the Duke with tears running down my face and said, yes.

I cried all of the time he was gone. The two days passed Grandma and the staff wanted to help me but I keep to my self, to keep me busy. I was not a happy eleven years old. the second day came, I went down to the castle wall and waited for The Duke after Three hours. The Duchess sent Martin (he is the youngest son of the duchess's personal maid Mariana) to get me. When I saw Martin coming, I asked him if he was going to wait with me, Martin said,

"No and the duchess sent me to get you, the Duchess wanted to talk to you and I should ask you to go to see her in her sitting room.

I was getting hungry and colder I didn't protest but I still didn't want to go Martin said, "The Duchess wants to talk to you and to come with him to see the Duchess

I went with Martin. I didn't want to cry in front of him, I went to see Grandma. As we walked down the long hall to the setting room Martin left me and went back to work. I knocked and the Duchess said to come in. I open the large wooden carved door. Went in. Grandma was alone sitting on her chase lounge. The phone was on a small table near the chase lounge. As I walked up to her, I was crying again. She told me to sit next to her. As I sat, she held out her arms and I hugged her hard I asked her if I hurt her, she smiled and said no.

Grandma said that the Duke called and it will take longer he thought it would, to do all he has to do. Plus he is helping his friend Winston Churchill and will tell us all about it when he returns to the castle and he will be here as soon as possible. Grandma said when the duke comes home we will have a party.

When the Duke returned to the castle, The Duchess invited all the workers to the Castle for the party in the big hall. We all had a good time. Than the Duke called all the workers to attention and told them what he and Winston where going to do.

Because of the bombings Winston Churchill and King George VI asked The Duke and Duchess to help save the children from the South of England.

THE SECRET PLAN

The estate grounds would be turned into a campus of sorts with long dormitories that would hold about 100 children each. The entire building are to be numbered to identify them this will help the children when they arrive. There are other buildings, a schoolhouse, and a dinning hall. All the buildings were being built under large trees or away from open spaces and not close to one an other. no roads going to or from any of the buildings. Each dormitory had rooms for the Teachers and Cooks. The rest of each of the buildings used as dormitories had open space for the cots, one per child. Smaller buildings, one for supplies, one was a medical station. One other building that one was near the lake which is about a ten minute walk from the closes building, number five. It was used as a Laundry, bathhouse and a latrine. It wasn't used much in the winter. But a wood burning stove in the building helped . As with all of the other buildings. All the wet clothing was dried on rope lines hanging up inside the building. None of the buildings had windows for two reasons, first to make sure no light shown at night and second to keep the building warm.   It would seem that The Duke of Tyne and Winston Churchill had a lot of help planning the developing of this campus.

The camp had no name for this place except everyone called it The Campus. The reason for the site to be nondescript. Was that no one identify it on a map or by name. This as history would recall was brilliant. No one knew this place existed

When The Duke of Tyne came back from his last trip from seeing King George VI and by than Sir Winston Churchill and Lady Clementine Churchill, All or most of the buildings were done. The Duke told them to start sending small groups of children.

When the duke arrived, I ran to greet him, Grandma was not far behind, The Duke picked me up and hugged me, by than the Duchess was at his side and the three of us hugged each other we went into the Castle. The servants and workers were waiting to greet the Duke. They all clapped, The Duke smiled and thanked everyone then he gave a speech.

"We are at war and we will all have a job to do to make sure the grounds are keptclean, we do not want to attack attention to this area. The Duke told them what he and Sir Winston had planed for the children and the people who would be arriving by train, a few groups at a time as not to attack attention to this site. No one except the train master knew were they were going. The others who know is   King George, Sir Winston, and now you all of you.

No one is to talk about this to people who do not live on this estate, NO friends or relatives are to know. This is atop-secret mission to save the Children. Please keep every thing you see or hear to your self. Should you see or hear any thing out of the ordinary or suspicious, please run to me and tell me no matter how trivial you think it is. Let me know. I will judge what to do about it. You are not to do any thing but tell me. I hope you all understand how important this is to keep the children safe. If any of you have, any Questions please come to me and I will answer your question. Any time you feel you want to talk.

Soon all the buildings where finished and children and teachers and cooks began to arrive. The supplies were brought to the train station; we all went to pick up the children and supplies, in horse drawn wagons and carts. I had my own horse and cart The Duke gave them to me for my last Birthday.

Everything was working out according to plan the Duke sent a coded message to Sir Winston on all the events and the timetable they had worked on. The Duke gave Sir Winston the code name of the estate, "The Fairy Ring. " The Duchess though it was perfect and told The Duke, who in turn made it official and gave it to Sir Winston and the King. Grandma explained it to me; The Fairy Ring is a circle of mushrooms in a grassy area. I laughed and said "Grandma you're smart no wonder the Duke married you". She laughed and said not to tell the Duke that, and laughed again. Little did we know the name would live on well after the end of the war?

Education in wartime.

Work continued until the fall of 1940 .when everything was going well no time to play any more because the Duke told The Duchess to make sure that the staff's children and I had a classroom in the castle. Because we were older than the children in the Dormitories. The children of the castle staff and I became close, but Martin and the others much more than I. Martin always looked out for me. (I think the duke told him to keep an eye on me.) And I was glad. The war was still going on, now that the Americans where in England and helping King George and the people of England to hold back the Germans.

All the children in the Dukes care (three hundred) were all under ten years old. The caregivers who were here were the Teachers, Cooks, and

Maintenance people who came with the children, some were parents, others were relatives, and still others were volunteers. One of the Kings officers chooses who was to go with the children. They didn't want too many for security reasons .No children under five would be here because they required extra care which was hard to come by. Those children went to a relative's home out of the big cities or to farms in the country side.

My class mates in the castle knew that if it wasn't for me that they would not   came to school in the castle but in stead they would be going to the Fairy Ring School as it was called now by the children . And they loved the castle school.

CHAPTER TWO

▼

The Duke kept in touch with my father Wilfred, because he knew what was happening in the United States, The Dukes lawyers send reports to him all the time. There for he knew all about his children in America. And what they were doing, I don't think grandfather was spying on them but he wanted to make sure that the business he entrusted to them stayed profitable.

My father told the duke that He and his brothers started a new company with their brother-in-law John (Jack) Stewart in Texas, The new company is called HST Oil and Drilling Company Inc.(Heron, Stewart, and Tyne) and so far they are lucky and bought more land in Texas about 10,000 acres. Grandfather was pleased with them and said: when the war is finished he and the Duchess would be coming to the United States. To visit them and will bring Thomas William and some other people to help take care of him and the Duchess.

The Duke had information about Margaret Elizabeth's husband and his family. It seems that John Stewart's family is well known in Texas and Washington DC. When Jack (as he is known and prefers to be called) married Margaret Elizabeth, whose father is an English Duke, this by it self made a big impression on everyone in Texas and Washington DC.

The Duke and Duchess's, second son, Reginald Thomas married a New York woman named Ann Olympia. She was a widow of a New York Stock Exchange member, who was rich. That made Reggie's dream come true.

As for William Haven, he married Florence Mischuck a Connecticut woman with a son out of wed lock. The boy's name is Charles. William gave him the right to use his last name if he wanted to. But William's wife hasn't made up her mind to do. The boy uses his father's last name Lyneburg.

Time to make a big decision

The Duke asked my father if he made a decision about returning to England after the war.

My father said that he and his brothers are going to stay in the United States, and live there. He also said he and Joseph Paul talked it over and decided to give-up any claim to the Dukedom. But will retain their English citizenship and have duel citizenship. The Duke said he would get his lawyers in New York to do the necessary legal contracts drawn up for each of them to sign. There will also be legal papers for Reginald Thomas and William Haven to sign, Margret Elizabeth must sign some legal Documents and have a judge in New York certify and notarize all of the Documents. The signed Documents will than be recorded and filed by a clerk in New York's City Hall. A copy of all the documents that were recorded, Will than be taken by the Duke's lawyer, along with a set of originals and sent to the Duke's office in London, England. The address is, Kensington Church Street, London W8 United Kingdom. For the Duke's Barristers to review and make sure every Document is in accordance to British Laws and then it will be concluded by the English Courts.

This should take about 3 months. By than maybe the war should be coming to an end.

The Duke of Tyne, asked for a copy of all the Documents for his files and to go over them.

Now the Duke of Tyne will have a new heir to his Dukedom.

The Duke's face had a small smile as he hung up the phone, after this last call to the United States knowing full well it would happen. Now he had to talk to the Duchess and Thomas William.

When Thomas William's parents went to the United States, the Duchess made sure that I corresponded with my father and mother. When I received a letter from them I would go to the Dukes Library and call my Grandmother to come to hear what they wrote to me. The Duke never said any more about the next Duke of Tyne and I didn't want to know.

I studied hard as Grandfather asked and he would help me with my studies when he had time, he was busy with the care of the children at Fairy Ring, looking after the estate , keeping Sir Winston and King George informed and running the business's he owned. The Duchess would always be there for me with her warm smile, I spent a lot of time in the lower library most of it with Martin and the Duchess.

Martin and I would study and laugh a lot. When in 1944 I turned 15 years old and Martin turned 17years old, we talk about what was going to happen now to our education. I asked him what his family was going to do about sending him away to school. He said, "Thomas he would like to talk to the Duke about it, and would he Thomas William, Do him a favor and ask the Duke if he can see him in his library, I said that I would go there right now. I left the first floor library and ran to the Duke's library, I knocked and waited for the Duke to answer then he said, "Come in. I went and stood in front of his big desk and told him about my conversation with Martin and asked if it be all right if Martin can talk to him when he wasn't busy. The Duke looked up at me and smiled and said that when he was done with his work he would send for him. I thanked the Duke and left to tell Martin who was at the end of the long hall waiting for me, I guess I knew that the Duke had a plan for us when he smiled at me in the library. Later that day the Duke called Martin to his library, they may take about his education. He had talked to his parents about what will take place, and they agreed with the Duke. Now it was Martins turn to make a decision about what the Duke had in mind for the two of them, He asked Martin to get Thomas William and bring him back here with you. As Martin turned to go the Duke smiled as the big door closed. The Duke had plans for the two of them. He waited for each of them to make a choice as to who would make the first move as always the Duke had it all figured out before they even knew them selves.

As he was ready to start work again there was a knock at the door. Knowing who was at the door he pulled a file from his desk drew said, "Come in, the door opened and there they were looking nervous.

The Duke said," Come in and sit down on the divan, I have something to tell you both about your education, and this will be your decision as to what you want to do about it. When I'm finished you may ask any question you like. Any conversation we have in this room between the three of us will be only for us, no one else, it's up to you to talk about it or keep quit and say nothing, as I said I's your decision. First Martin your parents know about it but not you're other family members, it's your choice.

Each of you will be receiving a letter from the King of England, King George VI, I have the letters now. Both boys looked at each other in disbelieve and surprise then looked back at the Duke who by now was smiling and amused.

The Duke went on," After I inform you about what's going on I will give you the letters. I know you will have a lot of questions, but for now let's continue,"

"Thomas William you are the next inline to become the next Duke of Tyne. Your family has chosen not to return to England after the war. They have given up all their rights to the Dukedom of Tyne.

Next you will be going to further your education by going to college in the fall.

Now Martin Gibbons, You are to start your education this spring and will be going to Cambridge."

Now here are the Kings letters to you, at that the Duke opened the folder on his desk and handed each boy a sealed letter with the seal of King George VI.

Thomas William held his letter and looked at Martin who was sitting next to him. Martin was trying not to rip the envelop as he opened it, his hands were shaking bad, he handed it back to the Duke and said, "would you please do me the honor of opening this letter, I'm nervous. The Duke opened the letter with his silver letter open returned it to Martin who took out the letter and opened it and stated to read it.

He got to emotional and started to cry put the letter down without finishing it. The Duke handed Martin a clean napkin he took from the small table that held his tea cup.

All this time Thomas William had his letter open and was reading it, when he finished it he look up at Martin and was surprised to see him whipping his face and eyes. He turned to Martin and put his arm around him. By then the Duke was standing by the both of them. The Duke asked them if they wanted a cup of tea. "They answered yes." The Duke called the Duchess to order a pot of tea and have it brought to his library, and would the Duchess please serve the tea. The Duchess was not surprised since the Duke talked to her earlier and was trilled to see the boys in the Dukes library. When the Duchess arrived carrying large silver tray, with a large matching silver pot of hot tea, and 4 cups and saucers. The boys never noticed that this was planed. Because in making of English Tea it took about a half an hour to brew a pot of tea. After the Duchess served the tea, she sat across from them in the Dukes big leather chair.

Now that you have the Kings letter I'll try to explain why all this came about.

For the last three years you two have done more than anyone of us. Everyone helped save the children but you also took care of the Stables and took the little children for horse back rides, When the teachers needed help and you were near you did it, and when the maintenance men needed a hand or a drink of water you two brought them liters of fresh spring water. No one asked you or ordered you to do that. It was things like that and many more, that all of us saw you do. You were not looking for a reward. this is what you received from a grateful King.

In my many reports to the now British Prime Minister Sir Winston Churchill I may have remarked about you two and how you made life easier for us during hard times.

Now they want to reward you, for your selfishness to the Fairy Ring Campus.

King George VI has given you free tuition to any college of your choosing for the rest of your educational life.

The Prime Minister Sir Winston Churchill has established a trust fund for you to use while going to school.

Upon your graduation Martin you will have a life time home here at our estate.

And The Duke and Duchess will supply you with a new automobile once you get your license to drive.

Now have you any thing to say?

The boys sat there and looked at each other, not believing what took place. And since it was Saturday, the Duke said we should have a little party.

The people on the estate had come to the Castle to honor the boys. And were in the big hall waiting for them and the Duke and Duchess.

When they arrived down on the first floor the Duke said to the boys to wait in the big hall while he went to get some wine from the wine cellar. Thomas knew something was about to happen as the Duke never got his own wine. But Martin went toward the big doors to the reception hall. Thomas called and said to wait for him. They opened the big wooden carved doors. A loud noise rushed at them, a lot of clapping and singing of "For He's A Jolly Good Fellow" rang out. The Duke and Duchess stood behind them as did Martins Mother and Father, Everyone was happy because the Duke had let it know about the letters from the King and Sir Winston.

CHAPTER THREE

▼

It was the next day when Thomas William and Martin got to be alone in the stable. Martin asked "did you know any thing about this" Thomas William looked at Martin and said" I had no idea any thing was going to happen. But I'm happy it did because you deserve every bit of it." Martin looked at me and smiled. I laughed because I though he would start to cry. And in his excitement he laughed. And we laughed hard we were full of joy.

Martin and I tried bringing ourselves to be serious. Martin asked "What college are you planning to go to"? "I'm going to go to Cambridge to look after you, I answered. We started to laugh again. We both knew and so did the Duke. We would be together at Cambridge.

Not because I'm next in line for the Dukedom but because we liked each other and we got along well, Martin was a big brother to me. We were happy about every thing that was happening to us.

I said after you get settled in at Cambridge and find your way around. I'll be coming down to make sure you don't screw up. And we laughed some more.

The day came to fast for Martin to leave and I was sad. The good thing was that the Duke and Duchess were taking the two of us.

First the Duke took us to register Martin Gibbons at the Trinity Hall, Cambridge. and get all the information and a list of all the books he will need, the Duke setup a checking account for Martin to use incase he needed some money. After the Duke had finished signing Martin in and making sure every thing was taking care of at Cambridge. The Duke said he had to go to his office in London, and to call him at the office when they were finished. The Duchess was going to take us shopping for clothes and supplies for both of us, we both needed a lot of school supplies. While we were shopping the Duchess took us to a restaurant because we were starving. While we were in the restaurant The Duchess showed us how to use the check book and told Martin that if he need any thing after we left to call her or the Duke.

We had to take two taxi's one taxi for Martin and his entire luggage filled with clothes and a large box of books and boxes of school supplies. And a taxi with the Duchess and me, and my luggage filled with clothes and supplies. I helped Martin bring all of the luggage and school supplies to his apartment which the Duke rented for him near Trinity Hall. Martin came back with me to say good-bye to the Duchess, She hugged him, and Martin and I looked at each other and shook hands even though I wanted to hug him, we said good-by. Martin turned and went up to his new apartment to settle in. and also he didn't want to cry. The Duchess and I waited for the Duke to pick us up at the University. The Duchess told me about The Dukes time at Pembroke College, Cambridge. The Duchess was going to a Private Girls School in London, the Duke was not a duke at the time, and he was in London on some business for his father The Duke of Tyne. And I was with some of my girl friends, we were in a restaurant in Piccadilly, and Thomas Eaton Heron was there with some of his friends as luck would have it, one of his friends by the name of Winston Churchill dared him to ask me for a date. Thomas Eaton came over to our table and introduced himself and "asked if he can talk to me for a minute and said to me, "that his friend dared him to ask the most beautiful woman in the restaurant if she cared to go on a date with him Mister Thomas Heron. Not being shy the Mistress Ellen Williams looked Mister Thomas Heron in his blue eyes and smiled and said nothing. Mister Thomas Heron asked Mistress Ellen Williams for her address. She reached for her purse opened it and took out a card with her name and address on it and gave it to Mister Thomas Heron and said, "That she wanted his card if he was serious. Mister Thomas Heron reached in to the inside of his tweed jacket and came out with a card for her. He asked Mistress Ellen Williams if she would do one more thing for him, would she wave to his friend with the big cigar. And the rest as they say is history. We laughed than the Duke arrived to take us home.

Martin was registered at Trinity Hall, Cambridge to study Law. He said that way he can keep helping all kinds of people rich or poor. The Duke and Duchess loved Martin's out look on life.

As time passed I couldn't make up my mind what I wanted to do in College. I talked to the Duchess about what she though I should do in College. She said that you should go to Pembroke College, Cambridge. That was the one that the Duke went to, and he should talk to The Duke about it. The Duchess is smart.

I went to see the Duke in his library and asked him that when he had some time I would like to talk to him about college. The Duke looked knowingly and said to come back in one hour and we can talk all we wanted to.

I went back to the Duchess and told her that I will be with the Duke in his library in and hour.

I had no place to go,

I went to the stables to saddle my horse and go for a ride around the estate, I hadn't done that since Martin left to go to college. I rode my horse Lux out of the stable and down passed the now empty campus building. The bombing had long since stopped, and little by little the now older children had returned to their families. The teachers and cooks went with them as chaperones. All of the maintenance men also left but a few stayed on to work for the Duke and to disable the large dormitories that were built for the children of "The Fairy Ring Campus".

As Lux hadn't been ridden by me for a long time I decided to go to the far end of the estate and than ride back slowly.

As Lux and I reached the end of estate we turned around Than I saw if I didn't hurry back I would be late for my meeting with the Duke. I slapped Lux on the rump and the horse took off fast I lost my balance and fell off and hit the ground face first. I was stunned and bleeding from my mouth. I grabbed my handkerchief and stuffed it into my mouth, clamed back onto Lux and took off back to the castle as fast as I dared. As I reached the stables Martin's father Howard saw me riding in and came to my aid. He called from the stable phone, The Duke answered and Mr. Gibbons told the Duke that I was bleeding. And was going to bring him to the castle Mr. Gibbons picked me up and carried me into the castle. The Duke and Duchess were coming down the stairs. The Duchess was horrified when she saw all the blood .The Duke told the maid to get some towels and warm water. The Duke wanted to see how bad the injury was, as the Duchess watched, Mr. Gibbons layer me on the floor and the maid returned with the towels the other maid had a basin and a pitcher of warm water. The Duke asked me if I was in a lot of pain, I shook my head no. The Duke now kneeing next to me said that he is going to remove the bloody Handkerchief from my mouth and to let him know if it hurt when he did. The Duke told me to open my mouth so he can remove the bloody handkerchief when he did get it all out of my mouth, the Duke could see no serious injury. Thomas William's front two teeth were damaged one was loose and the other one was hanging loose. The Duke reached into Thomas William's mouth and pulled out the tooth that was hanging. He asked one of the maids to get the First Aid Kit and bring it to him; in the mean time he asked the Duchess if she would clean her grandson's face. When the maid returned with the First Aid Kit she handed it to the Duke, he opened it and took out some gauze pads and put Thomas William's tooth in it and open Thomas William's hand and put the little package in his hand. By than The Duchess had Thomas William cleaned up. She looked sad; she bent over and kissed his forehead. The crowd around them smiled at the love The Duchess showed, even the Duke smiled. The Duke helped the Duchess up and asked Thomas William if he may stand, he said yes and The Duke and Duchess helped him up. The Duke asked the Duchess to call the doctor and hear what he had to say if they, should they bring him into the hospital to be checked out.

The Duke's doctor said, " to be on the safe side they should bring him to the Hospital in case there is something that we can't see."The Duke asked Howard Gibbons to bring the car around. The Duchess thanked everyone for their help and concern. At that all returned to their duties.

It took about two weeks for Thomas William's mouth to heal. Now he must see the Duke's Dentist

When the Dentist, Dr.Chancellor was finished with Thomas William he had the most beautiful smile you ever saw. The space that was there between his two front teeth was gone. When the Duke and Duchess saw Thomas William's new beautiful smile and how happy he was they knew that the Duke did the right thing by pulling the hanging tooth out of this mouth after his horse Lux threw him. Thomas William still loved that horse.

Thomas William wrote to Martin at collage and told Martin, What had happened he wrote that Thomas William was now much handsomer than Martin Gibbons.

I was lost without Martin; the estate was quiet no one was here, the, "Fairy Ring Campus "is no more.

I had to find something to do. It was about a week away from Christmas Day and everyone was busy. The castle was being decorated inside and outside. The aroma from the Kitchen was heavenly. Everything in the castle was shining even the floors were polished. There was nothing for me to do. I was thinking about taking a course at a local school to keep busy until I go to Cambridge.

I asked The Duchess, "can I go to a secondary school in Newcastle or Gateshead, both of them are close to the estate and if I had a license to drive I can get there and back in about 10 minutes. The Duke said that he would get me an automobile when I was old enough. now I'm almost 16 years old. I know how to drive because Mr. Gibbons showed me how to use and drive the farm equipment. I have been doing it since Martin left for college. The Duke said it was all right because that's how he learned how to drive.

The Duchess Smiled and knew what she had to tell Thomas William and he knew too. But he wanted the Duchess to talk to the Duke first. Thomas

William asked the Duchess to talk to The Duke. He didn't have to beg. He though that if the Duke know what he was up to it would be easier the get the Duke to say yes.

I received a call from the Duchess that the Duke wanted to talk to me. I didn't know if this was going to be good news or that I had to wait for another three months.

I went to see the Duke in his library. I stood out side those big wooden doors and said a little pray, I needed all the help I can get. I took a deep breath and knocked The Duke said "Come in Thomas William." I opened the door, look down as I entered than I look up to see the Duke Smiling. I tried to smile back but I was nervous I couldn't. The Duke said "Thomas William your Grandmother and I had a talk about your conversation with her, and since it was going to be a surprise for Christmas which is a week away you may as well know now there is no use keeping it a secret any longer. I want you to come with me to the garage.

As we left the Dukes Library I was hopping that my dream about an auto would come true. I was nervous and didn't notice any thing unusual around the castle as we were about to go to the garage Mariana the Duchess's maid came and said there was a important call for the Duke. The Duke turned to Thomas and said "Thomas William you go ahead to the garage and I'll meet you there when I' m finished with the call. Than the Duke turned and left to answer the phone. I stood there thinking something is wrong. I continued slowly walked to the garage. I didn't notice any thing happening around the court yard. I walking toward the garage. I heard someone call me from the stable I turned around and stood frozen to the spot were I was standing. It was Martin!! I couldn't believe my eyes.

He was running toward me. I went to him and we hugged. I asked what he was doing here. He said 'I'm on Christmas Holiday and got home when my father told me the Duke wanted me in the garage. That was than that I knew. I think we both knew. Than two garage doors opened and The Duke in one and Martins father Howard in the other one drove out of the garage in automobiles with bows on them. I look at Martin he stood there and couldn't believe what was happening. as the auto's approached us they stopped, shut off the engines and exited the auto's but left the doors open. The Duke and Mr. Gibbons smiled and looked at the boys and everyone came out of the garage and yelled "Merry Christmas." Than ran to the boys. and hugged them. I turned to Martin and asked, "You choose which auto you want? " We both laughed because the autos were the same a set of twins. As we approached the Auto's we can see our names were on the Drivers side of the auto along with the Duke of Tyne's Coat of Arms. Before we got in the autos Martin went over to the Duke and Duchess and hugged them and thanked them. As I was about to do the same thing, Martin came to me shook my hand and whispered "nice teeth." We both keeped laughing; keeping everyone wondering what was being said.

Than we got into the Autos started the engines. Martin rolled down his window and yelled for me to go first. I didn't hesitate I put the auto in gear and drove off slowly, went down the driveway followed by Martin. I can hear all of the people in the court yard yelling "hip, hip, and hooray". We weren't gone long about 5 minutes because we were excited I was afraid I would do something to the auto. And drove back to the castle Martin followed, I was waiting for him when he got out of the auto. I asked if he would care to have something to eat. He said he was starved, as we headed for the dinning room and asked the Duchess if we can get something to eat? She said to go to the dinning room and the cook is waiting for you both.

CHAPTER FOUR

▼

Martin and I talked the whole time he was home. He said that he loved college and that almost all of his class mates liked him. Some stayed away from the group that he was with. Martin asked Jason, his new friend in all of his classes, "What was their problem with Martin. Jason said," stay away from them because they think they own the college because their family history is in Cambridge.

Jason Maudslay's grandfather graduated from Trinity Hall and is an explorer. That is why Jason is here at Trinity Hall. Jason likes college because he is away from his three older sisters He calls them the three Witches from Shakespeare, Darkness, Chaos, and Conflict.

Some times they go to the library to study Martin loves the Law and is good at remembering a lot of information that he read in the library books. His grades were good. he helps Jason when he can.

He told Thomas William, that he couldn't wait to drive back to college to show off The Christmas Gift.

But most of all he couldn't wait for me Thomas William to start college and show up in the twin Automobile that should shut some mouths , and open some more. But mostly the two of them would be close by... They can see each other more often.

The time flew by fast and before they knew it, it was time for Martin to return to Trinity Hall.

Martin went to talk to the Duchess and asked her not to have a party for him because it would make it hard to leave Castle Tyne, and all the people. Tell them that he loved them and will miss them all. The Duchess knew what

Martin meant when he told her that and the Duchess agreed, than kissed him on his forehead.

Martin went to talk to the Duke, "Sir I can never repay you for all you have done for me and my family. The Duke was sitting behind his big desk in his library, got up and walked a round to Martin took his hand and Put his other hand around his shoulder and said, Martin you and Thomas William will never know how much the people of England own you for having the courage to give those children from," The Fairy Ring Campus a chance to grow up and have a better life. The Duke walked Martin to the big wooden door and shook his hand and said, "I'll be in touch with you when I go down to my office in London. In the mean time keep up the excellent work your doing with your studies and that will be my thank you.

Martin went to see if he could find Thomas William, but he was nowhere to be found. Martin got his luggage and went to the garage to put the luggage in the trunk and his Christmas gifts in the Automobile. When he opened the garage door he found Martin sitting in his own automobile. Martin walked over to Thomas William's Auto. And asked, "Why are you sitting in your automobile? "

Thomas William told him that he knew you would have to come to the garage to pack your Automobile, I have a gift for you and I didn't want anyone to know, it's between the two of us. Thomas William handed Martin a small gift wrapped box. Thomas William asked Martin not to open the gift now, but to wait until he was sitting in his apartment at Trinity Hall. You will know why when you open the box and read the letter Martin sensed that Thomas William was serious. Martin looked at Thomas William and said he would do as he asked. Martin loaded his auto. Than entered his Automobile. And put the gift on the set next to him, looked at Thomas William waved. Started the auto, and drove out of the garage.

When Martin entered is small but furnished apartment he carried his luggage into the bedroom opened the luggage and started hanging his clothes in the closet. Than went to the bath room and washed up.

Back in living room he took all the boxes of gifts that he received for Christmas opened them removed the gifts and put the empty boxes aside. When he was finished he had one more gift he had not opened until now. The gift Thomas William had given him. Martin held the gift in his hand before he took off the wrappings, opened the small box. Inside was a letter folded into a small square.

Martin unfolded the letter and started to read the note.

"My closest and best Friend,

Martin, I am giving you this Gift when you open the small Package at the bottom of the box you will know what it means, we grew up together and did everything together. I always thought of you as my big brother. Now I am asking you to be part of my life forever, as you may see by my gift this will make us part of each other. If you do not want to keep the gift you can return it to me."

Sincerely Thomas William

When I was talking to the Duke and Duchess a before Christmas, about taking a few classes in a local school, I had two reasons one to know more about some of the classes I'll be taking at Cambridge. And the second reason is to keep busy.

I wanted to talk to the Duke about the local schools and ask for his permission to go. I found the Duke in the stables with his horses as I approached the Duke, he looked up at me and asked "Thomas William if you are looking for something to do, get a brush and help me with Pembroke.

I said grandfather," I would like to go to a local school with your permission. And ask for your help in locating one."

The Duke looked amused and said he would make some inquires and come to his library tomorrow and we will talk more about it.

The next day I went to the Dukes library to meet with him. I knocked on the big wooden door and the Duke said, "Come in. "

I opened the door and went in and to my surprise, I saw the Duchess sitting near the Duke on the divan. I went to the Duchess and kissed her, she had that beautiful smile when she looked at me. I turned to the Duke who was standing by his desk. "Thomas William he said we are going to go to one of the schools that your father and I went to before we went to Cambridge. I think you will like it. Are you ready to go? "We all went to the garage to get the automobile.

I was pleased with the school the Duke and Duchess choose and that I would be going to start at a private school for 8 weeks, I was excited.

Princess Elizabeth comes to visit "The Fairy Ring Campus "

It was in 1943, the war was still going on in Europe but the bombing stopped in England. The Americans were in France and Italy and doing a good job on the Germans.

King George VI had asked Sir Winston Churchill and The Duke of Tyne what they though about sending Princess Elizabeth his oldest daughter to spend some time with the children at "The Fairy Ring Campus." They both agreed that it was a great Idea, a treat for the children and to show the teachers and everyone at the camp how much the people of England owned them for keeping their children safe and healthy.

It was planed to be a surprise for all the children. All adults were told to be prepared, and make sure all the children were ready and the dormitories were to be cleaned by all adults; the children were to be kept busy out side Thomas William and Martin Gibbons where to take charge of the children. The Duke was to be informed of any problem that may occur. Mr. Howard Gibbons was to clean the stables and the Dukes favorite horse, Pembroke, incase the Princess wanted to ride a horse. The Princess loves horses. Once every thing was ready as best it could be, it was a matter of waiting.

It was a beautiful late spring day when Princess Elizabeth arrived with her guards and some of her staff. The Duke had one of his staff at the railroad station to call him when the Princess arrived. No one knew what train she would be on or what time she would arrive. The Duke also had some Automobiles waiting for the Princess and her entourage

When the Princess's automobile drove up to the Castle court yard she smiled and waved to all the castle staff. Who were there to greet her?

The Duke and Duchess knew Princess Elizabeth as they had met before in London at Winsor Castle along with the King And Queen. The Duke bowed and the Duchess curtsied when Princess Elizabeth approached them, as the Duke talked to the Princess and introduced his grandson Thomas William he bowed and smiled at the Princess. The Duchess asked the Princess, "would you care for tea now or after the tour? " The Princess said, "After the tour Thank you."

The group walked to the "Fairy Ring Campus" First they went to the dormitories, then to the school. There she met the teachers and volunteers, Chatted with them for a little while. As they approached the stables the duke asked the Princess if she would care to ride one of the horses and he pointed out Pembroke to her as they both walked over to the horse Thomas William and Martin smiled at each other knowing he would. The Princess declined with a smile and said, "at and other time. "The Duke introduced Mr. Howard Gibbons and his son Martin Gibbons. The Duke explained to the Princess that Martin and his grandson Thomas William are the two boys who basically keep every thing running smoothly they help everyone, Teaches, Cooks, Maintenance Men and Volunteers. And still go to school.

The Duke said that they would now meet all the children who have been waiting patiently to meet Princess Elizabeth.

When the group was walking to the area where the children were, she asked Thomas William and Martin to explain how everything ran smoothly.

Martin Gibbons explained, "Each dormitory has a different time to get up, because there is not enough room in the washroom and toilet area to accommodate all the children at the same time. This is done on a rotating monthly basis.

There is one daily schedule to follow for everyone here. The schedule is written by the teachers. And posted on the bulletin board in what the children call the "Canteen ". (The Cafeteria)Each dormitory is numbered, each child knows his or her dormitory number, that number is used for everything that goes on here during the day.

On some days it may be necessary to change the daily schedule in that case we will all work together to make the adjustment. Today is a good example. As the group approached the children they began to sing, "Welcome Princess Elizabeth, Welcome to The Fairy Ring Campus. Than they all sang the English National Anthem, "God Save the King."The Princess went with Thomas William and Martin Gibbons to meet the children. The boys form two lines of children so they could shake her hand and say a word if they choose. This worked out well.

After all the children had finished talking to the Princess, Thomas William and Martin had all the children get their blankets and set them on the lawn for the picnic with Princess Elizabeth.

The Duke asked the Princess if she would care to have lunch indoors. The Princess said, "I would like to have lunch with the children on a blanket. "With that Thomas William rushed off and retuned with a new blanket, spread it out on the ground with the help of Martin.

The cooks made variety of sandwiches and served with your choice of tea or lemon ade and sweet biscuits and fruit.

The picnic went extremely well, all had a wonderful day with the Princess.

Now it was time for Princess Elizabeth to leave. The Princess thanked everyone and said, "This was one of the best days she had in a long time and was delighted to meet all of the children, and all the wonderful people who take care of the children of England. The Duke and Duchess Thanked the Princess for coming and shearing her time here with all of them.

The Princess went over to Thomas William and Martin Gibbons thanked them personally and said, "The Duke was right, when he said you two did a fantastic job I hope some day to meet them in London."

The Princess turned and waved to everyone, entered the Automobile and was gone.

CHAPTER FIVE

▼

In 1945 The Germans surrender to the Joy and Happiness of the people of Europe, But all important to the British people.

That Spring I had finished the eight weeks of classes at the Local school that the Duke and my father went to. Now I was ready to go to Pembroke College, Cambridge.

I was excited about starting College and seeing Martin, meeting new people and of being independent. But aware of the distinguished name I had to live up to.

Everyone at the estate had known I would be going to the same college that my grandfather had gone to; The Duke was proud and happy that I had chosen Pembroke. I don't think he had any idea about what was going to happen in a year from now, no one knew, least of all Martin and I.

The day grew closer to my leaving, the Duke called me to his library, told me to," sit down in the chair next to his desk." I did as he asked looking at him knowing that The Duke was going to inform me all about Pembroke College.

The Duke started by saying, "it was time for him, the Duke to let me, Thomas William know what to think about at the college the first year. "If the school should call my first assistant in London, Medford Walker, I'll give you all the information and phone numbers, Martin has just about all of them but not all, you will see why when you read the list."

The Duke Said "that since I went through the same educational system, he wants me to know what will be happening and be prepared to make the right decisions. Do not let other students influence you in anyway. If you have any doubts what's ever call me. I will be spending more time at my office in

London, because of the war ending. You call Medford, and he will do one of two things help you or get me to call you back. I have one more bit of information for you, you ask Martin about it, and I talked to him about sex. This will make it easer for Martin and you to talk about than you and I.

The day before I was to depart for Pembroke, the Duchess had a small party for me. The Duke couldn't be here because he was busy now that the war was comming to an end. He called me at the party and said that he would be in touch with me, after I get to college and settled in, the apartment was ready for me and if I needed any thing to ask Martin for help. He said he would to talk to the Duchess now and said good bye. I handed the phone to the Duchess and said, "The Duke would to talk to you. " After the Duchess talked to the Duke she said she had a gift for me from the Duke. The Duchess went to the Dukes library and came back with a package.

Now that was a surprise to me. I opened the package and was stunned to see a blazer. The Duchess helped me put it on; over the jacket top pocket was the Coat of Arms of the Duke of Tyne.

The Duchess said how wonderful and handsome I looked, and that the Duke had a closet full of them in all kinds of colors, and for any occasion. This is the first of many that you will have to ware, but you will always remember this one.

Grandmother helped me pack my clothes and get ready to depart in the morning.

The Duchess was sad to see me go, but happy for me knowing I would be getting a good education to carry on the Family name and business. The Duchess knew all about the Dukedom.

The next day the Duchess called Mr. Gibbons to carry Thomas William's luggage to his auto. And help Thomas William pack the auto.

I ran to the Duchess and hugged and kissed her good bye. Mr. Gibbons held the automobile door for me as I got in I thanked him, he shook my hand and told me to say hello to his son Martin for all of the people here who miss him.

I had called ahead to Martin that I was coming, "asked where I should park the auto when I get to Cambridge? "

Martin told me to park at Trinity Hall than we would go to Pembroke. He would wait for me out side and show me.

As I got there he was smiling and waving than I saw why he asked me to come to Trinity Hall, a group of his friends were there waiting for me to arrive in the twin. I parked and got out of the auto; men crowed around the twin automobiles and started to give a cheer. I didn't know if the cheer was for me or the autos. I would say for the automobiles.

Than Martin came over to me and shook my hand and smiled. He than introduced me to his friends. I guess Martin had told them who I was, and what college at Cambridge I was going to.

Martin said that he and I had to unpack his Jaguar. Get him settled into his apartment. Once that was done Martin had to go to class.

Martin showed me about everything he in the short time he had because he didn't want to be late for his class.

The first thing I did was to look around the apartment, everything that I needed was here, I started to unpack and put away, and arrange my clothes in the closet that The Duchess showed me how to do. Because no one was there to pickup after me, since I was the heir to the dukedom I had to keep my appearance well groomed.

I had to put away my books, get out my important papers and money than store them in safe place. I look all over the apartment. I found a loose floor board in the clothes closet. I tugged at it until it came loose than forced the board up. To my surprise but shocked some papers and money under the floor board. Removed the papers and wondered who put them there. I almost fell over when I read the first page.

It read, Thomas, I knew you would find this spot to keep your personal papers because this is where I kept all of mine. I had this apartment when I went here to school. Here is a list of thing you should keep in mind when you are questioned about our relatives. First know the person who is asking the question, Tell that person who is asking as little as possible. If they demand to know, you ask why they want to know? If they don't give you a satisfactory answer walk away, or refer them to the Chancellor.

There will be a lot of students and people who will want to be your friend when they find out who you are, be careful who you pick as close friends, I chose the students that were in my classes or the friends I trusted to help me. You have an advantage because you have Martin to look out for you. Don't give anyone a reason to dislike you they will have their own reasons. Always show respect to all the people you meet and they will return that respect to you. Don't be superior be your self you will go far being Thomas William

When you are finished put the board back and cover it with your empty luggage and shoe boxes or any thing else you want.

I though about what my Grandfather wrote and was glad that he got this apartment for me. I sat on the floor and opened the map The Duke left for me to study to get a round the campus with out any help. I started to wash up when the phone rang, it was Martin he said he would come by to see my apartment and to have a talk; he wanted to know how all the people were back at the castle. He would be here in about five minutes than we get something to eat.

When Martin arrived I finished changing into a pair of old pants and a sweater.

Martin knocked on the door. I went to open it as I was combing my hair. I greeted him with a big smile and a hand shake he walked in and looked around the apartment and said that he liked it. Don't change a thing, laughed and looked at me and said that we had to talk. I said ok do you want to stay here or go out and walk around out side? Martin said, "Out side it's nice out".

Out side I let him do all the talking because I had little to say. Martin started by saying, "that the Duke came to see him last week; we had a long talk about you. He also gave me a key to your apartment. Incase you get locked out, I'll have a key. The Duke is not worried about you; he wants you to know that I'll be here for you and to guide you if you need help. Martin said that the Duke had a talk with you about Pembroke and who to trust and who not to trust. He wants me to talk you on picking your friends because you trust everyone. When I see you are headed for trouble I have to stop you. Are you willing to go along with all that I and the Duke worked out for you? I looked at Martin and said yes. With that he smiled and sighed, reached over to me and hugged me. I said "may I say something", Martin nodded his head yes. "I want you and the Duke to know that I appreciate all the care you are giving to me. Martin said he knew.

Now for the good news and fringe benefits that come along with this package.

The Duke told you Thomas William about how he wanted me to talk to you about sex. And what to do about it when you are ready I will show you.

Here is how it will work out, The Duke has system worked out for us," you and I to go to see a few girls at a place were they take care of us. I have been their ,Martin smiled saying that. If you want me to explain the process Iwill. Or I take you there tomorrow and show you, it's Saturday and I have no classes. What do you want to do?

"Martin I think it's to early ,I'm not use to all this yet Let me get settled first than I'll let you know. Is that alright with you?"

Martin said, "let's go eat I'll show you where to get some good food. Do you have any money?"

The Duke left me a welcome to Cambridge package plus I have some of my own from home. As we headed for my Jaguar Martin asked me how the Jaguar rode down here.

I said it was great how about yours? Martin said about the same. We started to laugh. It felt good.

I started to get my class room assignments, when I reported to freshman's office. The office staff where helpful, they told me where to go and how to get there and the times the classes started. I was instructed to make sure I read and under stood the colleges Rules and Regulation that was in the package that every freshman gets.

The main rule is not to be late for a class. Once the classroom door is closed no one enters and you will be marked as absent. Should you be absent four (4) times in a month with out being sick or ill you will be penalized and expelled from that class. You must report to the General Board for a hearing.

If you are expelled from two classes in a six (6) month period you are to go before the Regent House for disciplinary action.

My major is Social Science and Humanities.

I will be going to class in Economics: economics is a social science to analyze and describe the production, distribuion, and consumption of wealth. Economics is Greek for relatives household, estate management of the state.

Social Science: The sum total of many things taken together.

Political Science: Discipline that deals with the theory and practice of politics.

Aristotle wrote in one of his books, "that man is a political animal."

Public Administration: The development, implementation and study of branches of government, (Policy).

Going to my first economics class I was nervous; entering the classroom I went to meet the instructor, Processor Russell, I asked what were the rules for the students in his classroom He gave me a fast ordination, told me to sit any where. I followed this routine in the rest of my new classes; it worked well with all of other instructors.

As the days went by I seen Martin, he was busy with his studies.

I met and got to know a lot of my classmate, as Martin told me a few will avoid me. that was no surprise. That didn't bother me at all.

I met and liked two students who where in all of the same classes I was, one was Christopher Smart the other is Elmont Hobs. We got along well.

Studying in the library with Christopher and Elmont helped each of us to get good reports on our classroom studies. Chris (that's what he asked us to call him) was good at economics. Chris always had a fast smile, and loved to tell jokes which kept us laughing all the time. Elmont on the other hand was serious and worried about his class report. We both told him not to worry much we would help him.

CHAPTER SIX

▼

When I turned 17 years old, Martin said "it was time for me to meet some of the girls. You will come with me now. You ask me any questions you want to, as I drive you to the Mansion (that is the name all of the male students call it). No matter whom you see there you do not talk to them there or when you see them at school, should that person talk to you nod your head nothing else. When we get there we will knock on the front door and will greet us and take us to a drawing room for us to wait for the girls to come in and stand before us, and tell us their names. You will pick the one you want, she than comes over to you and put out her hand to you. You will greet her and go with her to her room. How you react to her in the room is your business.

The girls have a different routine that they follow.go along with the girl. You may tell her it's your "first time "or not but I think she will know that and treat you with care. Thomas William the important thing to remember is to put on a condom. All of the time the girl will put the condom on you, or you may do it your self. But make sure you use one always. It's for your protection. For two reasons, first to protect you from getting a venereal disease and second The Duke will disown me and you if you get a venereal disease. The girls here are clean and are checked by doctors. When the Duke was going to Pembroke, he used to come here, that is why he told me to bring you here. No one is to know about this it would make head lines in the papers. You do not tell a soul in your classes or any where else. Never admit you where here ,Thomas William you have a responsibility to keep a clean image for the Duke and Duchess they love you much. The Duke knows and trusts you to keep a low profile in these matters.

Now let's go in and see the girls.

Martin knocked, a perfictly dress woman answered the door and said, "Good evening Gentleman, and welcome, come in. The woman looked at Martin and smiled and said, "Follow me." As we walked through the big vestibule, I was awed by how big the Mansion was. The Hugh marble staircase curved and got wider as it came down to the vestibule.

I followed Martin and the woman to a large room, when the woman opened the door and motioned us to go in; she asked Martin if he had a specific woman in mind Martin answered yes. Martin turned to me and said to choose a chair and wait for him as he had to talk to the woman. They walked to a small desk at the far end of the room, after a minute or two of talking Martin returned to where Thomas William was seated and sat next to him. Martin told Thomas William that he had setup a code name for him if this woman did not answer the door. If someone else answered, he would be shown in but asked for his name.

Thomas William was to say T.W.T and that's all and than follow his host to a room to wait for the girls, or the one he wanted. Thomas William asked what T.W.T stood for? Martin said it was code for billing purposes The Duke made it up for him. Thomas William Tyne. Martin and Thomas William laughed. Thomas William said it was a good thing his second name wasn't Nicholas. They both laughed harder.

Francis, Uris, and Nancy entered the room together; Martin got up to greet the girls. Thomas William stayed seated not knowing what to do. The four of them walked over to Thomas William.

Smiling Martin said to Thomas William, as he went to each girl. This is your first choice her name is Fran. Fran had black hair cut short, about 23 years old. Red lipstick and green eyes and petty

The second choice is Uris; Uris had auburn long hair (reddish brown) is about 21 years old, pink lipstick and brown eyes.

Third is Nancy, Nancy is about 19years old, long blond hair, blue eyes and bright red lipstick.

Martin knew which one Thomas William would pick to be his first sex partner. Thomas William got out of his chair and went over to Nancy and smiled. Nancy took his hand and led him out of the room. Martin was left with two of the girls he took them both. And laughed and thanked his benefactor and left the room with the two smiling girls.

Thomas William came through the door first all smiles looking for Martin. It had been a bout an hour since he had gone upstairs with Nancy to her beautiful room. When they were in the room Nancy closed the door, walked over to the large canopied bed and turned the covers down. She turned to me and asked if I would to shower first to help to relax me. I said yes. At which point Nancy took me by my hand to the lavatory, the lavatory had a large bathtub, with a shower, a toilet and a bidet. Nancy came over to me and told me to sit on the chaise lounge and remove my shoes. This I did as fast as I Than she told me to stand up, came over to me and started to unbutton my jacket removed it and set it on the chaise lounge than unbuckled my belt, unzipped my pants and pulled them down, at this point I started to get excided she look at me with wide shinning eyes. And a big smile, and said that she was going to enjoy this even more. Nancy said, "you are good looking and from what I see big too " I was surprised at what she said no one ever said that to me before, I though she was saying that to make me feel good. When I was naked and Nancy removed her dress she was also naked. We got in the tub and she turned on the shower and waited until the water was warm, not hot. This was wonderful.

After the shower Nancy led me to the canopied bed told me to lay down. And that she would do everything and relax. Which wasn't easy? Nancy was looking through a bed side table drawer said she was looking for a large size condom to put on me.

Now I no longer was a virgin. When we were finished we went back to the lavatory and showered and laughed as Nancy washed me all over. I got dressed as Nancy made a phone call; she said that someone would be here to take me back down stairs to meet my friend.

Now sitting waiting for Martin I knew why the Duke did all of this for me.

It was the same thing he went through.

Martin came in pleased with himself. I got up to meet him and headed for the door as our host guided us out.

Once we were out said and headed for his Jaguar, I looked at Martin and said, "That was the best thing that ever happed to me." Martin said laughing him too.

A Big Surprise

Both Martin and I were doing excellent school work at our studies and our marks are above average. I think the Duke gets all the information from the school on our academics and performance in class and on campus, and discusses them with the Duchess, and Martin's parents.

The Duke called me one night when I was studying in my apartment. He said, "He wanted to see me and Martin this Saturday in his new office, he wanted to talk to the both of us. He had talked to Martin and that I should call him now and make some arraignments to come to London. I told the Duke that I would and said good-by.

I called Martin; I guess he was waiting for the call. He answered fast. We wondering what was important, I said I didn't know. we made arraignments to meet and drive down in my Jaguar, about 10:00 A.M. Saturday morning

Driving down to London Martin asked, "Thomas William have you been to the Mansion?" I answered, "Yes and how about you, he smiled and said he had. I said," It's a beautiful place." We started laughing again, we know what we where thinking.

I drove up to the new Tyne Towers and parked in one of the reserved spaces, Martin and I went into the lobby where a security person. I went up to him and introduced my self. He said, "The Duke was waiting for them and to go right up to the Dukes office.

Getting off the elevator and walking to the glass doors with the Company name and logo in gold lettering on the door. Looked beautiful it read: TYNE CONSTRUTION COMPANY AND ASSOCIATES. Medford Walker was waiting for us, we pulled the glass doors open and walked up to Medford shook his hand and said were here to see the Duke. Medford said he knew and he would show us the way to the conference room and that the Duke was waiting for them. Reaching the conference room Medford opened the large wooden doors. As we entered I saw the Duchess sitting there. Than an empty chair and the Duke. I walked over to the Duchess and kissed her she hugged me and told me to get something from the side bar, tea and sweet rolls, I kissed her again. Turned to the Duke and hugged him and said, "This is a beautiful building". He smiled and said, "Yes it is but it's not finished, there is more work to do than he will have a ribbon cutting ceremony."

By than Martin was next to the Duchess and kissed her hand, she hugged him and kissed his forehead. After I got my cup of tea I sat between the Duke and Duchess in the empty chair. Martin also had a cup of tea. The Duchess said not to eat much because they going to have lunch when the Duke was finished talking. Martin was sitting next to the Duke.

First of all the Duchess looking at Martin said that she had talked to his mother and father about what the Duke was going to say. Martin looked surprised .

The Duke started, "Thomas William, Martin I have been in touch with the college and made the necessary arrangements to have a tutor for each of you to help you keep up with your studies. As we travel to the United States. We will be going before your summer school break. Since I will be doing a lot of business and The Duchess will be with our other children and grand children you will have a lot of free time to meet Thomas William's cousins. We will be talking more when I get more information. The three of us will be traveling to each of my businesses and I will be introducing you to all the people that work at that office.They will get to know you. I have plans for both of you to help me run the business. Martin you will be mine and Thomas William's Lawyer in the United States and England. That's if you want the position. You don't have to give me an answer now but think about it. And of course Thomas William you know some day you will be taking over everything as the Duke of Tyne. Both the Duchess and I believe you are the best ones for the work may talk about it or not it's no secret. But keep in mind it's still three months away I want to give you both time to prepare for it.

When we finished our tea the Duchess asked if we were ready for lunch. I looked a Martin and laughed and said we were starved, everyone in the room laughed.

The Duke said, park your Jaguar here and come with us and we will bring you back here to get your as the Americans call it car.

CHAPTER SEVEN

▼

When we got back to Cambridge, we were excited and bursting with happiness at everything the Duke told us. I talked to Martin for the longest time about his plans and what did he have in mined for his future. He said he would have to change a couple of courses, add International Law to his studies, and add other year before he gets his law degree. This would mean that we would be graduating together. Moreover, that would mean that Martin was smarter than Thomas William was. He would be an International Lawyer, and Thomas William would be The Duke of Tyne. We both laughed and couldn't stop we were crying we laughed.

A few days later while at school a messenger came with a letter from the King of England for me I didn't know what to do I called Martin and he said he had received a messenger also. and asked if I read mine I said no I asked if he read his he said no and that he would be right over to your apartment, than we will open them together. While waiting for Martin to get here I called the Duke to ask if he knew what this was all about. He said no but he had a good idea. and after they read the letter to call him, than Martin came in with is letter breathing hard he ran the whole way over here the Duke said to stay online and both of you read your letters. Martin opened his first and read his fast I don't think he knew what he was reading. When I read mine, I sat on the floor. Cried, Martin collapsed next to me and we hugged each other and forgot about the Duke on the phone. We started to yell aloud the Duke got nervous after I calmed down I picked up the phone and read the letter to the Duke

The Letter

I, King George VI, I want to thank you Thomas William Heron and you Martin Gibbons on behalf of the people of England, for your heroic deeds over a three year period. At the Duke of Tyne's estate and a campus called The Fairy Ring.

You both showed a steadfast and protective feeling for the three hundred (300) children in your care.

My daughter Princess Elizabeth who was there and seen first hand how you Thomas William and you Martin Gibbons, made the children of the Fairy Ring Campus, safe and happy even though they were far away from their parents.

Who were under great stress during the German Bombings? Still knowing their children were safe and healthy.

Thomas William Heron;
Martin Gibbons;

You are heroes to those parents but also all of the British people.
You will be receiving a Letter from the Ceremonial Secretariat.
Thank you, from a grateful King of England.

Sign; King George VI of England   This day April 12, 1949

I asked the Duke what this was all about. He answered, "Thomas William, Martin I need both of you to hear me". They both said yes shearing the phone. The Duke went on; "Sir Winston Churchill called me and said he was going to recommend the King should honour you both for your dedication to the children during the war. I think King George VI will knight you both and I think that Princess Elizabeth had something to do with this. She liked you two a lot after seeing how you handled the children. Other thing I had nothing to do with this happening. Nevertheless, I'm not surprised. I'm proud of you both

Martin would you care to call your relatives and tell them? On the other hand, would you prefer the Duchess call them?

Martin said that he would call his mother and father. I would enjoy if the Duchess to tell the rest of the household that would make her happy.

Thomas William asked the Duke if he knew when all this would take place? He said no. You will have to wait for the letter from the Ceremonial Secretariat's office.

Now you two will be in demand by the media because there will be a story about the rescue of the children during the war in all the British papers and you must inform the Cambridge Chancellor, as they may want to make arrangements for the security of the college and you.

Cambridge became overjoyed that not one but two of their students were to be knighted. Everyone was buzzing about it. Not sure who they were. Thomas William or Martin did not confess to anyone no one knew for sure who he or she was. The chancellor called Thomas William and Martin to his office. He wanted to set up safety rules for them and the college once their story appeared in the newspapers, the reporters would be all over the place looking to interview them. The chancellor would not allow the reports to disrupt the campus for the other students.

Thomas William was surprised by all the commotion that this letter had caused and who told them about the letter, he and Martin though it must be someone in the chancellor's office because he was the one who Martin and Thomas William had informed. Thomas William was sure that the Duke had talked to the Vice-Chancellor because the Vice-Chancellor had not talked to either one of them, Martin or Thomas William.

The two of them kept a low profile as long as possible and went to their classes and studied not saying a word, this would later hurt the boys who they were close to and studied with, when the newspapers came out with their names. Thomas William and Martin explained to their friends why they did not tell them it was to protect them. The Chancellor had asked them not to tell the students. They were bursting to tell everyone, but had to keep quiet.

The Letter from the Ceremonial Secretariat had arrived; Thomas William called the Duke and wanted The Duke to read the letter that arrangement would be made. Thomas William would talk to Martin and ask him to come with him to the Dukes office in London.

Thomas William called Martin and asked him if he would to come with him to the Dukes office and if he did would he call the chancellor and ask if they can go to London and talk to the Duke. In addition, inform the chancellor about the letters from the Ceremonial Secretariat. Martin said yes to everything and that he would take care of everything and get back to Thomas William as soon as possible.

Martin came to Thomas William's apartment and told him that he had gone to see the Chancellor and let him read the letter from the Ceremonial Secretariat. And that Thomas William and him had to go to London to talk to the Duke of Tyne about the arrangements that the Ceremonial Secretariat had made for them to meet the King George VI. The Chancellor had agreed to let them go, but make sure to let him know what will be happening. Martin told him he would ask the Duke to call his office and inform them what steps he will arrange for the ceremony.

Martin and Thomas William than took Thomas William's letter and Martin's letter from the Ceremonial Secretariat to show the Duke along with the letters from King George VI. Jumped in Thomas William's Jaguar and took off to see the Duke.

Arriving at Tyne Towers, Thomas William parked in the reserved parking and went into the new now completed office building. The security person at the new desk asked them to please come forward she would make their badges that they must wear at all times in the building. These are orders from the President of Tyne Construction Company, no one is allowed to enter with out a badge in the building, the badge must be worn on the out side of your clothing at all times. Martin stepped foreword and gave her his name. Martin read her name badge and said "Alison Gerail, what information do you need from me?" Alison looked up at Martin and smiled. "What is you first and last name and please spell them for me if you would. Martin spelled his name for her. After typing his badge card and inserting it in a plastic holder with a clip to attach it to lapel, Alison gave it to Martin with a smile. Than Thomas William stepped foreword, gave her is name and started to spell it Alison looked up and gave him a big smile and asked if he was related to the President of the Company, Thomas William smiled and said, " the Duke is my grandfather. Alison typed his card inserted it in to a plastic holder and handed it to him. Thomas William asked if she would call the Duke and tell him we are in the lobby. Alison dialled the phone and explained to who answered who was here. She hung up and said please go up. When they arrived at the Dukes office Medford said, "Your grandfather is waiting for you in his office I'll show you in. Martin said thank you I smiled at Martin but said nothing.

The Duke was on the phone when we were ushered in by Medford once in Medford closed the door. The Duke made a motion for us to sit down. He handed me the phone and said it's your grandmother she would love to talk to you.

I said hello Grandmother picturing her smiling, She said, "Thomas William I'm happy for you and Martin and looking foreword to hugging and kissing both of us, she said she knows we have a lot to talk about let me say hello to Martin," with that I handed the phone to Martin an told him The Duchess wants to say a quit hello.

I took out the letters and handed them to my Grandfather. He opened the one from the King first, read it and put it on his huge glass toped desk, Martin had finished talking to The Duchess and handed the phone to the Duke and he hung-up the phone. Now Martin had his letters in his hand ready to give them to the Duke. The Duke took Martin's letters read them and looked at both of us and got up from his chair came around his new desk, went over to Martin and as he got close Martin got up the Duke said how proud he was of him he hugged Martin, turned to me and hugged me and kissed my forehead wiped his eyes and returned to his chair took all the letters and said, "I'm going to have these framed for each of you if you have no objections."

The Duke started, "according to the Ceremonial Secretariat's letter The Knighthood Accolade will take place a Buckingham Palace on June 6th of this year starting at 11:00 A.M.. the Ceremony should take about two hours depending on how many will be Knighted, I had Sir Winston check on it for me and he said we will be the only two. Because it's now known as D-Day it be changed and made longer and a bigger celebration and more dignitaries.

Martin, you may have your relatives there It's up to you and your Mother and Father. After the ceremony is over, we will be going to a mansion that I purchased a long time a go and about finished renovating it for the Duchess and me now that I spend a lot of time in London. I was keeping it as surprise for the Duchess but now she will always know that it was for her on the day of her Grandson's Knighthood. Now she come down to London and decorates it her way.

We all go the United States as planned.

The Duke asked if we had any questions."

I looked at Martin and said to the Duke, "are you going to have a guest list for the reception at the mansion?"

The Duke said, "That is a good idea. I'll ask my building manager to get me a count on how many people the mansion will hold when finished. I know off hand you may ask a few of your closest friends at college to come, today if you want to but hold back on the number for now this is April we will have two months to get it right I hope.

No Guests will be invited to the Accolade at Buckingham Palace that is reserved for mothers and father; I will have Medford to get someone to make up maps and directions to the mansion. In addition, have them sent out with the invitations. The Duchess will take care of the invitations. Give the Duchess all the names and address if you can.

Martin do you have any questions?

"Yes, since we will all be down here on June 6th, will we getting our passports here in London?" for our trip to the United States?"

A good question I almost forgot about the passports, Thank You Martin.

I will get the application for you Martin, one for your mother also you may fill it out, and your mother will sign it. Than all we will have to do is have, your pictures take for the passports.

Martin asked why my mother would need a passport. The Duke answered because she is coming with us. I guess we forgot to tell you with every thing going on around here. Martin was shocked and said, "When you go on vacation you know how to travel, they all laughed.

CHAPTER EIGHT

▼

The day after the Ceremonial letter was sent to us. The Ceremonial Secretariat arranged to have a publication of the award in The London Gazette. It is usual for the award to be published giving details of the act for which he or she will receive the award.

Christopher Smart and Elmont Hobs, friends and classmates of mine came to me at school and wanted to know all about the story in the papers. First, I told them that reporters would be after them asking questions. Moreover, the answers they gave will be published in all the papers, be careful how they answer because the Chancellor will be looking at all the information given to the reporters. He did not want any negative image of Cambridge in the news. Now I'm sorry I didn't tell you before but, the chancellor asked both Martin and I not to say anything, Until it appeared in the papers because he wanted time to have the campus security ready for the reporters and news people, they are not allowed on the campus.

Now the good news, I am inviting you both to a reception at my Grandfathers mansion in London. You will be getting an invitation in the mail. I will need your full name and address the one here at school or the home address.

Here is how it all came to being; at the end of last week both Martin and I received a letter carried by a massager from the King of England, King George VI. In the letter the King Thanked both Martin and I for our work with the 300 hundred children during the war. We helped care for them at the Duke of Tyne's estate a camp of sorts called by its code name, " The Fairy Ring Campus," this was, to keep the location a secret. The Germans would not bomb it, as it worked out we were successful. No one knew were the camp was except the King, Sir Winston Churchill and the people who lived and worked at the estate.

We received a letter from the Ceremonial Secretariat's office informing us of the Knighthood and when it will take place and where.

The date is June 6th of this year at Buckingham Palace at 11:00 A.M. the ceremony should take about two hours. The ceremony at Buckingham Palace is for relatives. If you come to the reception, there will be a map in the invitation to show you how to get there.

Thomas William asked if they had any more questions. Elmont and Christopher looked at each other said no and thanked Thomas William.

A few days after the ceremony and reception, the whole group of us will be leaving for The United States. For some pleasure, but business.

As Thomas William and Martin entered each classroom for the next two days they was greeted with a Hip, Hip, and Hooray even the group that wasn't too fond of them clapped. Thomas William acknowledged each of his classmates and thanked them.

Because the reporter was not allowed on campus, they did not approach Thomas William. One did make it onto the campus with the help of a graduate student but was appended and removed from the campus.

Trying to keep his mind off the approaching events. Thomas William kept busy by studying harder. He called Martin and asked him how he was doing? Martin said he was coping and studying to keep his mind off every thing but that it was hard to do. Martin said, "He would be glad when it was all over and things would get back to normal." I said, "Martin thing will never be normal for us any more we will have to learn to adjust. Martin said I guess your right, keep in touch. Hung up.

A week before the events The Duke called both boys and said he is sending a car for them and asked them were to meet the driver that way no reporters bother them. Martin told the Duke to send the driver to the Chancellor's office that way no one will be suspicious. The Duke said, "There are a few items that I have to discuss, and he would see them at the mansion. Since this will be the first time for them to be here they need to familiarize them selves with the mansion. The Duchess and Martin's mother are here and will have some food for them.

We were waiting in the main building where the Chancellors and Vice-Chancellors offices are for the car to arrive. When the Vice- Chancellor came to us and said,

"The Duke called to get permission to let the limo pick you up here, of course I said yes. I want to congratulate you on both the fine leadership and hard work you both did for the children of England. One of them was my nice Isabella. I don't think you would recognize her now she is a teenager. Since I didn't know about your passed history I would have thanked sooner, we here at Cambridge are proud of both of you. You are both a great asset to the college. Your modesty shows why Sir Winston Churchill recommended you for this honour I would to shake you hands on behalf of my niece Isabella. Good job men.

When the limo arrived, we both Thanked the Vice-Chancellor, excused our selves and waved good by from the driveway, got in the limo and sat back in the over sized seats. Drove off to see the Duke.

Trying to keep track of where we were going we would find our own way to the mansion on our own, driving through London was to say the least, a nightmare. As we passed a large sign that read Carney Island. I asked the driver if we were close, he said almost there, another sign read Castle Point Golf Course. The street sign read Carney Way. The driver said, "That's the mansion as we drove closer I saw the big beautiful white marble building with four tall pillars also made of marble. I looked at Martin and said what do you think? He said that it's a nice cabin. We both laughed and did the driver. Martin said to the driver, "is there a name for the mansion yet?" He said he had no idea and to ask the owner when we get inside. Exiting the limousine, we walked up to the large alabaster carved doors. Rang the doorbell, waited for minute when the door opens two of the wonderful and beautiful women in the world waiting to us. The Duchess and Mariana, Martins mother we ran inside, hugged, and kissed each of them. Tears in everyone's eyes. Mariana said that she would see to lunch and the Duchess would take you both to the Ducks home office. Thomas William said I'm surprised she didn't say library. Things sure have changed."

As the Duchess grab each of us one on each side of her she showed us to the Duke's Home Office.

As we entered the office looking around I see why the Duke called this large room his office mumbled Thomas William. The large room was every bit an office. Nothing resembled the castles library, the furnishings were all new. As we went into the room I looked at Martin who looked surprised. The Duke told us to sit anywhere. When the lunch is ready, the Duchess will call us.

"First let me ask you both a question. What do you plan to wear to the Accolade Ceremony?" We both sat there in complete silence, shaking our heads Thomas William didn't open his mouth, Martin looked dumbfounded than said," we never gave it a though. The Duke smiled and said, "one minute."

He picked up the pickup the phone pushed one button on a key pad and talked to someone and said I think they are ready, the office doors opened and there stood

The Duchess and Martin's mother came in with some large boxes. The duchess came over to Thomas William, he got out of his chair and she said these are for you. Mariana Martins mother went over to Martin and before she reached him, he was out of his chair and at her side. She kissed him again and handed him the box, in the mean time the Duchess said to some of the help bring in the rest of the boxes.

A line of people came in with boxes and more boxes. Still holding the box that was given to them, they stood in awe. The Duke said, "Sit on the floor and open the boxes. I opened the box the Duchess gave me, removed the tissue paper to reveal the most beautiful Midnight Black Tuxedo Jacket you ever saw. The small pocket next to the left lapel had the Coat of Arms of the Duke of Tyne embroidered on it. The jacket had a white silk lining with my name also embroidered on the inside pocket. I couldn't wait to put on the Tuxedo jacket but the mirrors in the Dukes office were to small to see how the jacket looked on me. Grandmother came over to me and said turn around. All in the room clapped their approval. The duchess said the tailor is here and waiting for you and Martin to see if the midnight black tuxedo need to be altered.

Now Martin was standing and smiling with his identical Midnight Black Tuxedo embroidering and all. The Duchess said it was time to have lunch and called the workers in and told them to take the boxes to each of the boy's rooms.

After lunch, the tailor will fit the boys. As for now, we will go the kitchen-dinning room and have lunch. The duchess explained the formal dinning hall was being prepared for the reception.

At the kitchen-dinning room the five of us The Duke, The Duchess, Mariana Martins Mother, Martin and I sat as the Duke outlined how the Ceremonial day has been planed.

We will be awakened early to have breakfast, start to get dressed making sure to look in the bedroom mirrors to make sure every button is buttoned, every zipper is zipped, and do not put anything into your pockets boys except your handkerchief.

Once we get to Buckingham Palace, we will be escorted into the Throne Room.

You two will be escorted to an anti room off the throne room to wait for the escorts to accompany you to the throne room.

The Kings Pages in the Throne Room will seat the families. There will be invited guests and sometimes the Royal Family.

The Knighting Ceremony

After all the guests are seated and before King George VI enters, Thomas William and Martin Gibbons you will be accompanied in by the Lord of the Chamber, once you reach your seats do not sit down. You will keep standing and wait for The Royal Family members to enter, The Lord of the Chamber will tell you what to do, follow his instructions. He will announce The Royal Family Members at that point all assembled will stand. Than The Lord of the Chamber will announce King George VI. Once the King is seated, the Lord of the Chamber will tell the guests to be seated. You will keep standing until told to sit by the Lord of the Chamber.

When everyone is seated, he will tell you to sit.

The Duke explained, "You will see the Throne where King George VI will sit. There are three steps and the Throne Platform on the step below the platform a palace page will place the knighting-stool on the step below the throne platform, when called to do so. When you are called by the Lord of the Chamber you will stand up bow to the King keep standing and wait for instructions from him he will than approach you ask you your name, turn to the King, bow and announce to the King. The knight-elect Thomas William Heron Grandson of The Duke of Tyne is present to receive the Accolade.

Martin Gibbon, son of Mr. Howard and Mrs. Marians Gibbons is present to receive the Accolade.

At that point, the Lord of the Chamber reads the Proclamation from the Ceremonial Secretariat written by the Prime Minister Sir Winston Churchill to King George VI for his approval. King George VI accepts the Proclamation.

The Lord of the Chamber turns to the Palace Page and asks for the Knighting- Stool to be placed on the third step after the Knighting-stool has been put in place and the page returns to his position King George VI will ask you to step up and kneel the ceremonial Sword is brought to the King by a person chosen by the King.

In this, case it maybe Princess Elizabeth

First, the King George VI lays the flat side of the sword's blade onto the accolade's right shoulder, than raises the sword gently over the accolade's head and places it on the left shoulder. The new Knight stands up after being promoted

King George VI presents the new Knight with a medal on a chain. The Knight bows his head as the King places it around his neck. It is the order of King George VI for Gallantly of Extremely High Order. This is a new

Order, Thomas William and Martin Gibbons you are the first to receive this award.

This is the same processes that will follow when it's your turn Martin. This should make it easier for you Martin, now that Thomas William showed you what not to do. And they all laughed.

CHAPTER NINE

▼

June 6, 1946

The morning of the Knighting day (as I call it) I didn't feel any different than any other day, I got out of bed, took a shower, brushed my teeth, combed my blond hair (I had a hair cut yesterday) looked in the mirror and liked what I saw. Went into the bedroom put on my under wear and socks a pair of pants and a sweater. No shoes. Went next door to Martins Room and knocked and told him to get his ass out of bed. To my surprise he answered to come in. I opened the door and went in he was sitting on the bed dressed in jeans and a shirt, shoes and a nervous smile. I asked if he was coming to breakfast? He said yes as he got off the bed and came over to me. He stood there looking at me for a minute and said, "I think you were right about things will never be normal again." Than we hugged, walk down the hall together to the marble stair case. The marble stair case, reminded me of another stair case I seen in another mansion and smiled. Martin looked at me and wanted to know what I was smiling about. I told him what I was thinking, he laughed and than we started to laugh out loud. As we reached the bottom of the stairs the Duke was standing there and heard us laughing. The Duke said, "You two are in a good mood I 'm glad to see every thing should go well today. Come and have some breakfast with me. They went into the Kitchen-Dining room.

The Duchess and Mariana and her husband Howard were eating. We all said, "Good Morning." Sat down and Matthew the new butler the Duchess has engaged for the mansion asked what we would care for, for breakfast? I answered a cup of black coffee no sugar no cream. Martin asked for a cup of tea. The Duchess asked Thomas William about his choice of coffee. Thomas William explained, "At school in the morning I need something fast and hot I couldn't wait for the tea to brew I started drinking coffee on my way to class or the library." The Duke looked at the Duchess shook his hear and continued to drink his tea the duchess had made for him. Martin and I laughed than everyone laughed.

After Breakfast the Duke told everyone to be ready by 10:00 O'clock. The Limousines will be waiting for us. Thomas William and Martin and his parents will be with the Duchess and me in one limousine the other family members will be in the other limousine.

The Duchess had asked Matthew to help Thomas William and Martin to get dressed and to make sure all was done properly. By 9:30 A.M. Matthew had both boys dressed and were told not to sit down until the time to get into the Limousine.

When they came down to the foyer everyone was waiting for them, taking pictures. The boys looked like they stepped out of a magazine. They were handsome. The Duke and Duchess were beaming as were Mr. and Mrs. Gibbons.

After getting into the limousine the boys we told to sit in the back of the limousine than Matthew closed the limo door and told the driver to pull up. The next limousine pulled up and the Duke and Duchess got into that limousine than Mr. and Mrs. Gibbons also got in with the Duke And Duchess then Matthew closed the limo door. And they were off. Leaving Thomas William and Martin wondering what the hell was going on than Martin said your Grandfather had this all planed for us. He's a great person I love him. Thomas William looked at Martin and said he did too.

As the limousines crossed over Vauxhall Street Bridge we turned on to Rochester Row a police car and some police motorcycles surrounded all the limousines. I turned to Martin and asked, "What the hell is going on now," It's the Duke again". Said Martin, as we turned on to Artillery Row we could see a lot of people up ahead on both sides of Birdcage Walk. I said, "I suppose that's the Duke too."

The motorcade had to slow down the crowd was big I though at first the King was coming. Than the driver turned to us and said that the people want to see you two men to thank you for what you did for their children. Smile and wave don't open the windows or we will never get to Buckingham Palace. We did as the driver suggested. People were hollering our names there were signs reading Thank You and God Bless You. There must be thousands of people here wavering the British Flag.

We made it to the gates of Buckingham Palace, the police had to clear the way for us and keep the crowd back so we could drive in. once inside the driver said do not get out. The Palace Guards will open the limousine door when all the limousines are in the court yard. You will wait for the other people to get out of their limousines, and then the Palace Guards will open your doors you will get out of the limousine one from the right and one from the left. You will stand there until the limousines pull away. Than the two of you may join the others, at the Palace Steps. And wave to the crowd

The palace information officer was waiting for us at the top of the steps He said we have 15 minutes to get inside and be seated. He turned to Thomas William and Martin and said, "I will explain a few things to you about what will be happening. They all went inside and the information officer told one of the Palace Pages to escort the others to the Throne Room. Thomas William step forward, you will be going first to be Knighted, than you Martin.

Now come with me to the antechamber. Now all you're the guests may be seated. You will be last to enter the Throne Room. Once the ceremony starts no one may enter the Throne Room.

The Palace Guards will escort you to the Throne Room and open the doors for you. The Lord of the Chamber will greet you and softly ask you to identify your selves Thomas William you will quietly tell him your full name, Martin you will do the same. the Lord of the Chamber will than turn and proceed down the isle, Martin you will follow behind him than Thomas William you will follow Martin (you will see way when the Lord of the Chamber stops and nods to you) there are two chairs reserved for you when the Lord of the Chamber nods to you Martin you will turn right and stand in front of the second reserved chair. Thomas William you will turn right and stand in front of the first empty chair. When Princess Elizabeth enters she will enter through the same side door as the King. When the princess is in place the Lord of the Chamber will announce King George VI.

When that is said the entire assembled Guest will stand as King George VI enters and keeps standing until the King is seated.

From there on you will be instructed by the Lord of the Chamber. Keep an eye on him at all times and listen closely to him. Should any thing occur? Not planed for watch the Lord of the Chamber, he will instruct you what to do. OK!!

Are there any questions? I want to also thank you for what you did for our children and I want to shake your hands. He came to each of us and shook our hands and said God bless you both. There was a knock on the door, he opened it and a Palace Guard said it was time. As they held the door open we exited the room and followed the guards to the Throne Room doors, they opened the throne room doors. We approached the Lord of the Chamber. He nodded to us leaned forward and asked us our full names. We told the Lord of the Chamber our names. The Lord of the Chamber turned and proceeds to walk down the aisle, Martin followed him than I followed Martin. When the Lord of the Chamber stopped, Martin glanced to his right and saw the two chairs he looked at the Lord of the Chamber who than nodded. Martin turned right and walked to the second chair turned to face the Load of the Chamber and stood there. I looked at the Lord of the Chamber he nodded I turned and walked to the first chair turned to him. And stood there facing him. The lord of the Chamber announced Princess Elizabeth she was carrying a beautiful Sword and what looked like a chain on a royal blue cushion walked over to a small but elegant table placed the cushion with the sword and chain on the table and walked to a chair near the Throne. And stood by the throne. Than the Lord of the Chamber asked all to stand, announced King George the sixth of England. Everyone bowed as he entered and ascended the steps to the Throne then sat down. Princess Elizabeth was next to sit. The Lord of the Chamber asked everyone to sit. Thomas William and Martin did not sit. The Lord of the Chamber than bowed to the King. And announced to the King.

The Knight-elect Thomas William Heron, Grandson of The Duke and Duchess of Tyne is present to receive the Accolade.

The Knight-elect Martin Gibbons son of Mr. Howard and Mariana Gibbons is present to receive the Accolade.

Now they are told to sit by the Lord of the Chamber. Now at that point the Lord of the Chamber reads from the large book he was carrying.

This is a proclamation from the Ceremonial Secretariat written by The Prime Minister Sir Winston Churchill to King George VI for your approval.

King George VI said, "I accept the Proclamation."

The Lord of the Chamber turns to a Palace Page and asks for the Knighting-Stool to be placed on the Third step. After the Knighting-Stool has been put in place the page back away (Thomas William saw this and knew what he had to do) to his position.

The Lord of the Chamber asks the first Accolade to come forward.

Thomas William walks up to the Knighting-Stool and   kneels than King George VI and Princess Elizabeth; carrying the cushion and sword and two chains and medals stand before Thomas William, takes the sword from the cushion lays the flat of the sword's blade on to Thomas William's right shoulder than raises the swords gently over Thomas William's head and places it on his left shoulder. The king says arise Sir Thomas William Heron. He stands up and leans forward bows his head. The king has replaced the sword on the cushion than picks up the Chain with the medal attached to it and places the chain around Thomas William's neck. King George VI says, "This Medal is for your Gallantly of Extremely High Order. This is the King George VI Medal. Sir Thomas William Heron you and soon to be Sir Martin Gibbons are the First to receive this award.

Than the King leaned toward Thomas William and softly said, "We are happy to meet you after all these years; the British People truly own you and Martin more than I can say. Thank you. Princess Elizabeth stepped forward and thanked him and said that she is waiting for an invitation to go riding with them at the estate.

Thomas William Thanked the King and Princess Backed away down the steps and to his chair as he approached his chair he turned his head to see where is chair was and sat down. Martin saw all this and knew what he had to do.

The Lord of the Chamber opened the book and read the next name.

Knight-elect Mr. Martin Gibbon's son of Mr. Howard and Mrs. Mariana Gibbons is present to receive the Accolade.

Now the Lord of the Chamber reads the proclamation from the Ceremonial Secretariat, and than the Letter from Sir Winston Churchill to King George VI

For your approval The King said, "I accept the Proclamation. "

The Knighting-stool was still in place. The Lord of the Chamber asked second Accolade to come forward.

Martin's ceremony was exactly like Sir Thomas William's

After being knighted and receiving the Medal and Chain, Martin Thanked the King and the Princess backed down to his chair looked over his shoulder and sat down.

As soon as he sat down The King and the rest of the people in the Throne Room clapped a long time.

The Lord of the Chamber went to the Knights and congratulated them and said you two did every thing right the best he had ever seen in the many years he has been Lord of the Chamber. Shook their hands said to wait for the King and Princess to depart before they left their chairs. He moved to the side of the room and waited for the king to make his move. When he did he turned to all the people in the room and said please wait until Sir Thomas William and Sir Martin Gibbons have left the room before you move. The information officer was waiting for them as they exited the room and took them to the up stairs balcony so that the thousands of people could see them. The rest of the guests went in to the court yard and waited for them

When Sir Thomas William and Sir Martin appeared on the balcony there was a roar from the crowd that could be heard in the United States. The two Knights were awed by the thousands of people. They keep yelling and someone started to sing God Save the King. The King and The Queen appeared behind then as they turned to see the Royal Couple they bowed and split in two the King and Queen waved to the crowd, the King was standing next to Sir Thomas William and the Queen was standing next to Sir Martin. The King put his arm around Sir Thomas William, and the Queen hugged Sir Martin the crowd went wild, they kept yelling and singing wavering the British Flag. King George VI turned to Sir Thomas William spoke as loud as he dared and said, "This is to show you two how much appreciation they have for what you two that you did for three years of dedication to the Children of the Fairy Ring Campus. The Queen and I add our thanks along with them. The King And Queen waved one more time and left leaving the two knights waving at the Hugh crowd. The Palace Guards escorted them down from the balcony to the courtyard. Each one of the Invited Guests went up to the new Knights and congratulated them.

CHAPTER TEN

▼

When the last of the guests congratulated Sir Thomas William and Sir Martin the limousines appeared and waited for the new Knights, at this point the Duke had talked to Mr. and Mrs. Gibbons and they agreed to his plan. The Duke and Duchess with Sir Thomas William would go in the first limousine and Sir Martin would go in the other limousine with his parents.

There where many hundreds of people waiting to see the Knights. When the gates opened the police and the guards had a hard time getting the people to move. Finally the limousines moved through the gates and on to Birdcage Walk. The police cars and motorcycles guided them through the streets and to the mansion. The Duchess hugged her new knight and cried as did the Duke. We will talk later for now wave to the people. Sir Thomas William did as the Duke asked and enjoyed every minute of it and smiled and finally got to where there were no more crowds and got to the mansion. The Duke offered the driver a large tip but he said no it was a privilege for him to drive them. He wanted to shake Sir Thomas William's hand. Hearing this Sir Thomas William reached over and took the drivers hand and smiled. Than got out of the Limousine as the driver opened the door. The other limousine pulled up and the Duke went over to that limousine to give that driver a tip Sir Thomas William followed the Duke as Mr. and Mrs. Gibbons exited the limousine Sir Martin was out on the other side of the Limousine the driver opened that door first as Sir Martin had asked and shook the drivers hand and thanked him .That driver also refused the tip and waved good by as he pulled away.

Everyone went in side the mansion by now it was 2:30 in the afternoon. The reception is scheduled to start at 4:00 O'clock, we had some time to be alone and have something to eat. I asked the Grandmother for some food and drink for me and Sir Martin I asked, "Sir Martin would the Knight like something to eat before the joust begins." We all laughed, He answered, and "I'll have what the Nobel Knight Sir Thomas William is having."

The Guest list was amazing Sir Winston and Clementine Churchill, members of the Royal Family, other Dukes and Duchess'. The Duke said he had a few Special Guests that he was waiting for. The Duke had hired a photographer, Sir Martin and I keep posing on or by the beautiful marble staircase. At 6:00 O'clock the Duke said his Special Guests had finally arrived they were supposed to be here this morning but The American airlines were never on time like British Air. I knew who was coming. I couldn't wait when my Mother and Father came in the front door I was on the marble stair case posing for pictures. We ran to each other and hugged and kissed. My mother said she was happy for me and just like any mother said, "Thomas you have grown tall." Everyone in the foyer laughed and smiled, my father hugged me and kissed my forehead. Than my brother Joseph Paul came over and said, "Is it all right to call you what I called you when we were kids." "I said definitely no." Laughed again
I "said this is the best day of my life."
The Reception went on until 2: 00 P.M. in the morning. The food and drinks kept up to the demand, the Duke said no one should go home hungry or sober. Had called the news media they were kept out side of the gates, but the Duke had food and drinks brought out to them.
At 2:30 P.M. I looked for Sir Martin and found him with a beautiful movie star. And told him I was going to bed. He looked at me, said good night, Knight.
In the morning I got up and went down to the kitchen-dinning room to have a cup of coffee. The Duke and Duchess having breakfast alone. I asked where the rest of the family was the Duchess said they were at the Castle. They had a bad day trying to get out of New York because of bad weather and thunder storms. They wanted to relax. Mr. Gibbons volunteer to drive them there. He said he had to check on the castle and the stable, meaning the horses. He was a great help to the Duke.
I asked if Martin had come down to breakfast. The Duke said no. Matthew came in with my coffee and asked what I wanted for breakfast I asked the Duke what he had? He said two soft boiled eggs and toast. Now I shook my head and said, "I'll have some kippers and toast with strawberry jam. The Duke shook his head. And laughed
Now I want to get serious, "said Thomas William first I want to tell you both that I think you know how much I Love you, and 'I'll never leave you or the estate I want to thank you for making yesterday the most amazing day of

my life. And I know Martin will also agree," at that point Martin came in and said are you talking about me. I looked over and said I was thanking them for yesterday the most amazing day of our lives. Before he sat next to me he went over to the Duke and hugged him than kissed the Duchess came over to me sat and, "said how come I had to show you where to sit yesterday." "I said I would show you how to walk backwards down the steps with out falling." The four of us kept on laughing when Matthew came in with my coffee and asked Sir Martin what he would wanted for breakfast and waited for the laughter to stop, to eat. Martin asked what the Duke had before Matthew could answer we all laughed; Matthew continued two soft boiled eggs. Martin shook his head and said "two eggs over light and bacon orange juice and a cup of tea, would you bring the tea now please". The Duke couldn't hold it back any longer and said "what is the matter with soft boiled eggs".

By the time we stopped laughing my coffee was cold

After breakfast the Duke said we were all going to the castle and spends the day with Thomas William's mother and father. Than I will make the arrangements for our trip to the United States and ask my son, Wilfred to make arrangements for the three of us to see our business and maybe do some buying. I have a few ideas we will talk about it later let's get ready to go to the estate. When everyone is ready I will call for the car. Please have your luggage by the front door. The help is cleaning up after the mess you two made yesterday. He smiled.

When we arrived at the estate everyone was busy doing some thing. Martin and I found Joseph Paul in the stable, asked him if he would care to go riding with Martin and me, he said yes, after we saddled our horses we went riding to the edge of the estate when we were far enough from the castle Martin and I started to ask Joseph Paul a lot of questions about the United States and asked him to show us around when we get there. He said he would do that for us. Than Martin asked Joseph Paul if he would introduce us to some women, he looked at us and nodded smiled and said, "Definitely yes."

Than Martin, "asked Joseph Paul about Harvard Law School and what kind of law was he studying. He answered I'm torn between criminal justice and banking laws, my father wants me to go into banking law. I'll choose my major this fall when I go back to Harvard."

Joseph Paul "asked Martin what he was majoring in," he answered international law.

Than they turned to Thomas William, he said he wasn't majoring in anything because he would hire both of you to work for him. Than laughing they headed for the castle and some food.

We went to have lunch with my mother and father and everyone else who could make it?

Martin and I answered all the questions had about what took place here during the war. My father said that his brothers and his sister will see you in a while, that is way they did not come, which as it turned out was the best thing considering what happen to us. We felt bad about missing the ceremony but at least we made the reception. Joseph Paul, "said and I met a movie star I liked and made a date with her when we gat back to the U.S.A. My mother asked about the knighting ceremony, I said, "I don't remember to much about it except when King George VI leaned over to me and told me how much he liked me and what we did for the children, you know we had three hundred children here for three years. To tell you the truth I enjoyed all those children." "Martin said he did also but of course we were children at that time too that is why we didn't think of *not* doing it. Everyone on the estate at that time should be honoured the only thing is that of the people who came with the children from London were being paid by the government. We of course were not. We are getting paid now maybe not in money but in the love and gratitude of all the children and their parents those children are alive today because of what three heroic men did for them. They are The Duke of Tyne, Sir Winston Churchill, and King George VI." everyone agreed with Sir Martin.

Sir Thomas William said "that since yesterday was D-Day June 6th. It's still fresh in a lot of people's minds that added to the joy of the day. That is why thousands came out to see us and the King and Queen.

My mother and father came to me and said you have grown up to be an intelligent andgood looking young man. I thanked them and said you have to thank the Duke and Duchess for the way I grew up than I smiled and look at my mother.

She said I see the space in the two front teeth has closed and you have taken care of your teeth. I looked at both my mother and father, "said you should thank the Duke, he was the one who called the doctor after he pulled one of them out after I fell off my horse. Again everyone laughed.

I asked my father if he would care to have copies of the official photographs of the Knighting ceremony with me and the King. He said yes, he would hang it in his office. I think your Mother would like to have a set of all the pictures that were taken at the ceremony and at the reception. Your mother wants to show off and brag about her son the Knight to all the ladies she plays tennis with.

My father said that they would be returning to America Sunday he had to make arrangement for their arrival and to warn the people of the United States that they are going to be invaded by the English Knights of the Round Table. My father has the same funny sense of humour as his father The Duke of Tyne, now I know where I got mine from.

On Sunday morning we were having breakfast before my mother, father, and brother were to go home to the United States "I told them that I would miss them but this is my home and would always love them. My mother cried and my father said he under stood and will always be proud of him and can't wait to introduce me to all his friends in the United States. He will be the proudest and only father of a genuine good looking knight in New York and Connecticut maybe in all of the U.S.A." I didn't know if I should laugh or cry. I got out of my chair and went over to my father hugged him than to my mother and kissed her.

Arrangements for our trip to the United States was all set for June 23rd in about two weeks, Martin and I went to London to the Tyne World Headquarters as it was called now. To spend some time with the Duke going over the Businesses that Duke Industries owned in the United States.

As not to confuse some of the issues with the different businesses, the Duke Setup two offices near his office. One for Martin and one for me. He gave each of us two different stacks of files. One for me the other for Martin. We had regular offices with phones and filling cabinets our name plates on the out side of our door, my name plate read,

"Sir Thomas William Heron 'KGM' "

"Sir Martin's name plate read,

"Sir Martin Gibbons 'KGM' "

(The KGM means that we also received the "King George Medal" and are initialled to use it at the end of our names.)

He said to study the document and to make notes of any thing that they didn't under stand. My files were businesses in the United Kingdom. Martins were all those of business in the United States.

Stamped on the out side each file folder in big red letters was the word CONFIDENTIAL.

The Duke came in and asked Thomas William to call Martin and have him come in here. Thomas William did as the Duke asked. Martin was at the door. As he hung-up the phone. He knocked and came in.

The Duke said he had a few rules for us to follow, first as you see each file is marked confidential those are to be locked up in the filling cabinet at all times and only to be read one at a time the rest will be locked in the filling cabinet do not leave any files marked confidential in the open position if someone you are not sure of is in your office with you. Do not leave any confidential files on your desk if you leave your office for any reason. Always keep them under lock and key. We will be getting together later to go over your notes in my office, bring the files you have any questions about and your notes. Lock up the other files and leave the key with Medford. When you are finished with your notes and have the answers does not put them in the regular trash .There is a disposable unit in the mail room down the hall ask Medford to show you how to us it. I don't use it I have no knowledge about it

All this is necessary to keep our business secrets out of the competitors' hands.

There is millions of pounds worth of information in those files. Now get to work. The Duke turned around and left. When they were alone Martin said The Duke is a smart man. I'm glad I'm on his side. Martin turned and went back to his office with out and other word and left Thomas William standing there thinking.

CHAPTER ELEVEN

▼

Working with the Duke at the Tyne World Headquarters in London, living in the mansion was a great learning experience for Martin and me. When we finished at the headquarters at night we went to the mansion, The Duchess was there sometimes we would have dinner with her and the Duke if he was here and say how excited we were about learning and seeing how the Duke handles his business and treats his employees. That you cannot get out of a book. Life out side of the classroom is something you have to learn on your own. The Duchess would sit there and listen, say yes and no at the right times nod when she had to and smile at both of us. She was a Dream

Martin and I would talk about nothing but business most of the evenings after dinner sometimes with the others, sometimes the two of us. I would listen to Martin about international law. And he would listen to me on domestic business we learned the difference between English laws and American laws and how to sometimes get around them.

A few days before we were to go to for America, the Duke said "go back to the estate and do some packing for our trip and relax.

On the way to the estate, I said to Martin could we make one stop near Cambridge, I have to see someone. Martin asked who you know around there. I said Nancy. Martin said yes! Yes! Yes!

Everything is set for us to go tomorrow morning from the mansion in London. Make sure you have every item packed that you want to take, if you forget anything, don't worry. They have some nice stores in America ask the Duchess. We will be leaving the estate in about an hour. Sir Martin and Sir Thomas William will be in charge of packing the cars with the luggage, no tipping please. Alright boys get with it. We will stay the night in the mansion.

Mr. Gibbons will drive the Limousine with the Duchess, Mrs. Gibbons, and me. Martin or Thomas William will drive one of your Jaguars. Mr. Gibbons will drive our limousine back to the estate. And the Jaguar will stay in the mansion garage, in case one of us will have to come back ahead of the rest of us.

Getting up early and getting ready to leave for the airport was no problem this will be our first time on an airplane for Martin and me. I was a little nervous. I called Martin, he was up and was finishing getting dressed, and I told him I would meet him for breakfast. I was finished drinking my first cup of coffee when Martin came in. I asked if he was nervous, he said yes. He didn't want to talk much. I eat in silence and told him I was going to my room to brush my teeth and get my luggage and bring them down.

Than the rest of the travellers came for breakfast as I was leaving to get my luggage

The Duke told me that the Duchess's luggage and his luggage were ready to bring down. When you see Martin tell him to get his mother's luggage and bring them down. Than Martin came out of the dinning room I yelled get your mother's luggage. He looks at me and laughed and nodded.

When we were all set and the luggage was packed in the car. Howard Gibbons drove us to the airport.

After taking off the plane banked left to head over the Atlantic Ocean when the Duchess said "look out the window you can see the mansion. It looks like a white cliff in the morning haze." Now I had a name for the mansion. I leaned over to the Duke and said The Duchess did it again. Grandmother gave the mansion a name, White Cliff. He spoke to the Duchess and she smiled and said yes.

The plane ride was uneventful and we would be in New York in about 6 and half hours. Because of the tail winds.

Flying into New York and over Manhattan Island, the New York skyline was breath taking, it was beautiful, and I loved it. I asked Martin what he though about it. He looked at me and didn't say a word. I never said a thing about his fear of flying to him or anyone else. When we landed at Idyllwild Airport Martin was a changed person. He was relieved to be on the ground.

After going through customs and getting our luggage my father was waiting for us with his rented limousine to take us to Connecticut.

The airport was busy as soon as we got our luggage we headed for limousine; put our luggage in the car my father drove out of the airport on to the Van Wyck Express Way than to the Hutchinson Parkway to the Merritt Parkway into Connecticut than to New Canaan.

New Canaan, Connecticut is a small town over the New York/ Connecticut state line. The town is a village we have in England quiet not much there for residents to do. When you want good restaurants and entertainment in 5 minutes you can be in the centre of Time Square in Manhattan.

The limousine pulled up to a large Tudor style house my father had rented for us. We loved the house. Martin and I moved the entire luggage in to the entrance hall. The Duchess and Mariana went to check the kitchen and to see where everything was located. My father and Grandfather went to check out the rest of the house and the Duke assigned everyone to their rooms. The Duke called us to come to the back of the house to see our room. Martin and I will be sharing a large room with two large twin beds and a back door to the large swimming pool and patio area. My father told us where the other rooms were and who's room they were and to bring the luggage to the rooms than relax and go for a swim. After running to the front hall and getting the luggage delivered to the rooms, we remembered we had no swimsuits. I went to my father and asked were are the swimsuits he laughed and said there are new suites in the pool house next to the change rooms and showers near the patio. In five minutes they were in the pool.

My father told the Duke that after they settle in he will call and handed him a list of phone numbers for him to reach his other children. And the reason his sister couldn't be here is because her husband John Stewart was in the hospital and had an operation and was sick, and the Duchess could reach her at the numbers he had give the Duke. My father side he had to go now and had to get back to his office in New York, call his wife Irene if they needed any thing. She will be over as soon as she can in about an hour.

My father handed the Duke two sets of keys for the cars he rented that are in the garage.

Than he hugged the Duke and said he was glad he was here and left.

When my mother came to the house she had a large vase of flowers for the Duchess they were beautiful my Grandmother hugged my mother and thanked her. Called Mariana and said to put them on the dinning room table. The flowers looked beautiful in the dinning room. I asked my mother were Joseph Paul was? She said he was working for his father in New York and will be back in time for the party tonight. I said what party? My mother answered the family reunion at our house. Everyone will be there except Margret. Her husband John Stewart is in the hospital mother didn't know too much about the circumstance. Wilfred keeps in Constant touch with her. He gave the Duke her phone numbers for the Duchess to call when every thing has settled down here. Is there any thing you need now I'll take the boys to town and show them around and pick them up for you if you want us to? There are a couple of food stores a pharmacy and lots of small good restaurants in the canter of our small town and we love it this way no hustle or bustle. Mariana said she has a list for the Duchess to look over and add to it if need be. The told the boys to change into some thing presentable in case Irene wants to introduce you to some of her friends they meet in town. Martin and Thomas William did as the Duchess asked. Was backing in about 10 minutes looking every bit a knight.

Getting to town took about five minutes it was about 1:30 in the afternoon; the town was busy to my mother's surprise!! She met half of her friends and some had their daughters with them shopping for summer clothes they said. Mother introduced us as Sir Martin and Sir Thomas William of England, who were here to attend a family reunion they will be here for about a month. Some of the young women they met were and seamed impressed to meet us. And wanted to know how they were made Knights? What an opening line the boys had. The boys said to the ones they liked they would like to explain to them ,but had to get back to the Duchess of Tyne she was waiting for some of the items we had to buy for her. And may we call them when they were free? The women gave them their phone numbers and names. My smiling mother wrote their names and phone numbers on a pad she carried in her handbag; they stopped to have lunch at her favourite restaurant. More friends of mother's by the time we finished shopping for the Duchess we were back to the house at about 4:00 o'clock in the afternoon.

When we got back to the rented house Martin and I carried the bags of items the Duchess wanted in to the kitchen were Mariana was with The Duke and Duchess having a cup of tea. Mariana brought the tea with her that the Duke and Duchess liked from the estate in England.

Mother said she had to go to get everything ready for the party tonight. The boys would take one of the cars from the garage and follow her to their house so they know were it is and how to get there. Thomas William and Martin yes and asked the Duke for the keys to one of the cars. The Duke said the keys were on the table in the front hall. They got a set of keys and waited for Thomas William's mother to get to her car, Martin backed out of the garage and followed Mrs. Heron's car. The house wasn't far away maybe about three miles. It's easy to get there and back.

Martin and I were by or in the pool in the sun all the time, until it was time to get ready for the party when we were dressed we went to the living room to wait for the Duke and Duchess and Martins mother, the Duke who was dressed first came to us and said that he would drive one car with The Duchess and Mrs. Gibbons and we go in the other one.

When we got to my fathers house, a lot of cars parked in the large drive way. Martin and I waited for the three of them that we could all go in together

As we walked in my mother and father greeted us at the door and said that it was out on the patio around the pool and took us through the house to the back patio. As we entered everyone clapped. I was bewildered by it all and as was Martin. As the evening went on I called Joseph Paul aside and showed him the list our mother made up for Martin and me, he read it, I asked if he knew any of the girls? Joseph Paul said he had gone to New Canaan High School with some of them but didn't know a lot of them because he left for Harvard Law school right after high school. Not much for inside information.

The Duchess and Mrs. Gibbons had a great time at the party getting to renew acquaintances with the children and grand children. Mrs. Gibbons help raise them with the Duchess when they lived in England. They were both going to love staying here for about a month. The Duke, Martin, and I will travel around the United States checking on the other business the Duke owned or was partners in with my father and Jack Stewart.

The next morning at breakfast the Duke said that we were going to go to his New York Office to get acquainted with his small staff. The Duke said he will show us some of the things we read in the confidential files in England. We will be leaving in about a half an hour, in the limousine on the way to his office he gave us an itinerary of where and when we will be travelling, to meet his other employees and partners and to check on Jack Stewart in Texas.

At the office of Tyne Industries (the name of the Dukes companies in the United States) we met the staff of ten employees. Two of them were English and born in Nottingham, England. They were happy to meet us they read about us in the news here in America it was big news here too. The rest of the staff said you don't have to be English to honor a hero they patted us on our backs (I guess that's what Americans do!)

Martin, I and the Duke went over Tyne Industries business for about two hours and did not add any thing to the meeting asked questions which impressed them even the Duke, who smiled and said nothing.

The Duke called my father and said "Way don't he and Joseph Paul join them for lunch at the Plaza and after lunch go to his office. The Duke said he was buying, they said yes and they will meet us there. Than the Duke called the Plaza to reserve a table for five. In his name Duke of Tyne Thomas Heron.

The Duke told Martin to drive and he would give him the direction as they went.

When they got there the Duke told the Doorman to have the limousine parked and handed the doorman some money the doorman reached for the phone on the wall near him said to who ever answer to have a driver here now and park a limo. They went inside and saw that my father and Joseph Paul were waiting for them at a table. The Duke went up to the Maiter'd, spoke to him and handed him a large tip, we went in and. The dinning room was not crowed; a waiter came over and asked if they wanted any thing to drink the Duke ordered a bottle of champagne for all of us. An other waiter came over with the menus and told us, the soup of the day, catch of the day, left, than the champagne arrived with a tray of glass carried by and other waiter. After setting the glasses in front of each of us left the first waiter came over and pored the Duke a small portion for Duke to taste, nodded to the waiter who than pored each of us a glass put the bottle back in the bucket of ice and also left.

The Maiter'd come over and asked the Duke how the Don Perrier On was, the Duke nodded and the Maiter'd departed. We ordered our lunch; Joseph Paul asked Thomas William and Martin if they had any plans for tonight when we get back to New Canaan? We said no. he said well he would be at the Tudor about 7:30 / 8:00 o'clock to pick us up. We were overjoyed. After lunch we went to my father's office. There we sat around for about an hour while my father and the Duke talked about business. Martin drove the limousine back to New Canaan.

In the car on the way back the Duck said he had called his daughter Margret in Texas. She suggested that we come here as soon as possible her husband is not doing well and the medication is not working and she is worried about him.

She would like us to meet her adopted daughter Carol Heron Stewart; she is 18 years old now. The Duke and Duchess knew about the circumstances around the adoption. He explained; Margret and Jack had a live in housekeeper who had a baby girl out of wedlock and since Margret and Jack couldn't have any children they took care of the baby and the housekeeper. When the baby was 7 years old the mother Carol was killed by her jealous boy friend. He was shot by the police when he tried to shoot the police when they came to arrest him. That is why they adopted the baby they had raised her in their home, it was natural that she stay there. Jack's lawyer handled everything legal. Jack and Margret loved that child.

CHAPTER TWELVE

▼

When we arrived back in New Canaan the Duke said he was going to make reservations for our flight tomorrow morning .The Duchess told the Duke that Irene was taking care of it, they were planning to go Thursday afternoon and that Mrs. Gibbons will be staying here. The Duke called the air lines to make reservations for three first class tickets to Texas the first flight out in the morning and that it was a family emergency. He got three tickets for a 7:30 departure. Now they had to pack for the trip.

When Joseph Paul arrived to pick up Thomas William and Martin he had his girlfriend with him. He introduced her to everyone, Joseph Paul said this is Brooke Orr she is a senior at The Gunnery School in Washington, Connecticut. Brooke "said hi, nice to meet you all" they all got in to Joseph Paul's Cadillac and left.

The Duchess knocked on Thomas William's door to wake him up; it was 5:00 A.M. Tuesday morning he stirred, moved and "said ok I'm up."Than jumped up went into the bathroom to shower and the rest of his morning ritual after 10 minutes he came out got dressed pick up his luggage he pack yesterday and went to the Dinning room for breakfast, Mrs. Gibbons insisted on preparing. Martin came in at about the same time as the Duke. They sat in silence in the meantime the limousine arrived to take them to the airport. They eat fast and left thanking Mrs. Gibbon. Got into the Limo and went to Idyllwild Airport. They checked in at the TWA ticket counter and waited to board the plane. Thomas William looked at Martin and" said do you want a cup of tea from coffee counter?" Martin "said no thank you."

On the plane Thomas William was sitting next to Martin whispered "Is every thing ok? Is there anything I can do for you?" Martin shook his head no. Thomas William sitting between Martin and the Duke "asked His grandfather have you ever met Aunt Margret's Daughter Carol before."The Duke said "yes when she was much younger before the war, I think she was about 9or 10 years old. This will be the first time I have been back in the United States and Houston since 1941. I guess Carol would be about 17 or 18 now she was a little girl as I recall.

For the rest of the flight the Duke read the latest report he had received from his office in Houston

Margret and Jack lived about 20 minutes out side of Houston in Bay Town, Texas.

First the Duke wanted to stop at his office. His office wasn't far from the airport. After getting the car that the Duke had ordered, he drove to his office. Introduced us to his staff. He had 15 employees 10 where in the office, 5 were in the field checking on the refineries that his company owed Tyne Industries. Sitting in the conference room and listening to the Duke talk to his employees, made me think, he had different personality as a business man and that of a family man. Martin and I listened we did not read about this part of the business, I made a mental note to ask the Duke about this later. Two hours later we said our good bys and went to meet Margret and her family in Bay Town. We were greeted with hugs and kisses by my Aunt Margret.

Aunt Margret apologized for not going to our Knighting ceremony. Asked what she and her family should call us, how should we be introduced to other people? I said what ever you are comfortable with. She called her daughter Carol.

Carol this is your cousin Sir Thomas William and this is Sir Martin Gibbons, aren't they handsome Knights. Carol looked at Thomas William then at Martin and said "what do you do during the day." We broke up laughing.

I looked at Martin and could see that he was taken by her. She was beautiful.

With black hair olive white skin and the most beautiful red lips he ever saw. I think Martin was in love. His eyes were shining and he had the dumbest smile that didn't stop. Martin whispered to me if nothing else this trip was worth all the flights in the world. The jene-sais-quai was a bomb. Carol asked us what college did we attend I said I go to Pembroke College at Cambridge. Martin said he was studying Law at Trinity Hall, Cambridge. Carol looked at Martin and said maybe you can help me I sent in my application to Trinity Hall Cambridge about two months ago but I haven't heard from them. Mother wanted me to go there. Maybe my grandfather The Duke can help me I'm carrying a 4.5 average the top of my class. Martin stood there with his mouth open and couldn't speck.

Martin waited for the Duke to say something about helping her, than said to his Granddaughter. Your mother and I talked about this a last year and we both agreed to help you to get to know the British people and our family in England.

You have been accepted at Trinity Hall. Carol ran over to the Duke threw he arms around him and gave him a big kiss, than Turned to Martin hugged him and kissed me. I asked Carol what was she going to major in? She replied Arts and Humanities

I asked if we were going to visit Jack in the Hospital and aunt Margret said tomorrow because we have a lot to do today she has to talk to a few of his doctors and find out what they are going to do about his medicine He is not responding to it.

Carol said she has made plans for us at a local Seafood Restaurant which is on the Gulf of Mexico it's beautiful at sunset, looking at Martin she turned to Thomas William and said she had a date for him, her best friend Debbie, and her father is also in oil in fact everyone in Houston is in oil.

Carol asked her mother and grandfather to join them they said no, they had some business to take care of. Than maybe they would join us for a drink.

Carol said" that after Martin and Thomas William unpacked and got ready to go in about and hour or so then we will go pick up Debbie Rosé wall, Thomas William's Date ." "I asked who the date is for Martin". Carol said I am and smiled at Martin. Martin didn't say a word.

Martin and I shared a guest room and the Duke's room was next to ours. We went upstairs to unpack and shower, I hung up my suits and jackets in the closet while Martin lay on the bed in a dream and a smile on his face. I" asked aren't you going to get ready, Do you want me to tell Carol that you are not going?" Martin smiled, laughed and "said her.!!"

After the boys showered and dressed they were ready, Thomas William was wearing his blazer that the Duke and Duchess gave him, Martin wore his blazer that his parents gave him after he and Thomas William were knighted it had the King George VI Insignia on his breast pocket. They both looked dashing and commanded attention.

While waiting in the living room for Carol to come down. Aunt Margret came in and said she had to get a picture of the Knights to show off to her friends and Jacks family. Than Carol came in, she looked lovely she was wearing a white silk knee length dress with a red silk sash and red shoes, with her black hair and red lips she looked beautiful. Martin was breathless when he saw her. Thomas William nudged him to bring him back to earth. Aunt

Margret asked us to pose for pictures. First the three of us with Carol in the middle, Thomas William alone and Martin alone. The Duke walked in and was asked to pose with the three of them.

Thomas William asked "why that many pictures?" Carol's mother said she was going to show Houston and Texas what handsome Knights she has in her family.

When all the pictures were taken , the Duke call Thomas William aside said don't worry about the bill at the restaurant because his Aunt Margret is paying for everything, you thank her. As they were leaving Thomas William went to his Aunt hugged her and wisped thank you for everything she laughed and" said my husband has a lot of money. Now it's my turn to spend it on my family.

They all got into Carol's Cadillac, Carol asked Martin to drive and she would tell him the way. When they got to Debbie's house, the three of them went up to the front door, rang the bell and waited for someone to open the door. Carol said hello to the women who told them to come in. Carol introduced them to Mrs. Theresa Rose`well Debbie's mother. Mrs. Rose 'well was surprised to see how good they looked not like the cowboys she is used to seeing around here. When Debbie came in to the living room they were now in, Carol introduced her to first Sir Martin her date Sir Thomas William Mrs. Rose 'well "said please call me Theresa. And what should I call you." Martin said "you call me Martin and that's Thomas William. Debbie was a tall girl about the same height as Thomas William with blond hair and green eyes and a fast smile. They could feel that they were going to have a good time tonight. As they left they all said good by to Theresa got into the Cadillac and drove off. Carol gave Martin the directions on how to get to the restaurant.

Arriving at the restaurant they were greeted by a parking attendant. Got out of the car and went in side and was greeted by a receptionist and were told to follow her to their table which was in the back of the restaurant next to a large bay window. Walking to the table people were looking at them as they made their way through the restaurant Carol spoke to a few of the people she knew and nodded to a few others as did Debbie. When they got to the table the view was spectacular, Thomas William said it reminded him of the Duke And Duchess's White Cliffs mansion in London which over looks the English Channel. Carol and Debbie were chatting and did you see her or how jealous some of their old class mates were. Martin and Thomas William smiled and read the menu. Some of the girls they knew who were here come over to the table and said hello, Carol introduced the boys to the girls as Sir Thomas William and Sir Martin. The boys stood and shook there hands, and said glad to meet you. Carol and Debbie were overjoyed. Martin leaned over to Carol and wisped was this all planed? Carol said no but it couldn't have worked out better. Some of these people wouldn't even talk to me at school. We know it happens to us all the time said Martin.

Martin "asked if they knew why we were knighted."

Carol said something happened during the war?

Martin explained about The Fairy Ring Campus. Saving the three hundred children from the bombing, and caring for them for three and a half years.

Both Debbie and Carol were impressed. After eating and having some wine that the duke ordered for us. A small band started to play from a small stage. We asked the girls if they would care to dance they said yes. The music was slow and easy. The lights were low it was great when the song ended Carol went up to the band and talked to the band leader. In the mean time we went back to the table. The lights came up and Carol was at the microphone and was about to say some thing when I spotted the Duke And Aunt Margret standing in the entrance. We had no idea what she was going to do.

Carol started "When we came here tonight for some a fun. I wanted to show off my Cousin and my date. I though you should know why I wanted to show them off to you. Those gentleman are big hero's in England because of what they did for three hundred children and get this they took care of those children for three and a half years .while the Germans bombed their parents who were working in London and else where in England. Did not get paid for their 24hour days nor any monetary reward but I'll tell what they did get they received, the love of everyone in England and the King and Queen of England. That is why they are called Sir Thomas William Heron KGM and Sir Martin Gibbons KGM... The coat of Arms on their jackets is not ornaments they are the real thing. Stand up and be recognized Sir Thomas William my cousin And Sir Martin my date. The band started to play God Save the King.

Everyone including the waiters and waitress was standing. And clapping the Duke and Aunt Margret came over to the table than everyone came over to shake there hands. Sir Thomas William leaned over to Sir Martin said "I hope this doesn't happen every time we go out to eat.

CHAPTER THIRTEEN

▼

Aunt Margret drove us to the private care center where Jack Stewart was, making sure that he was getting the best care possible. Aunt Margret, Grandfather, and I went into see Jack while Martin and Carol stayed in the waiting room. Carol said that she and her mother were here all the time almost every day. Martin asked Carol if she would like a cup of coffee or tea. She said "a cup of tea with cream no sugar this surprised Martin he said "I though all Americans drank coffee? She smiled and replied "Don't forget my mother is English and that's all she drinks I got use to tea."Martin and Carol went to the cafeteria ordered two cups of tea. Thomas William came looking for them and ordered a cup of coffee. He didn't say anything about Jack, Carol's father. Carol finished her tea got up and told them she was going to see her father, and would be back in a few minutes. After she left Thomas William told Martin "it did not look good for Jack Stewart the doctors had him on a pain killer Morphine he has cancer is not expected to live long.

Carol and her mother came into the cafeteria the Duke was still with Jack. Thomas William asked his aunt if she wanted a cup of tea. She said" No thank you." Carol said that when the Duke came back they would all leave.

My mother and Grandmother arrived Thursday night, Carol and Aunt Margret went to pick them up at the Houston Airport. In the mean time Martin, the Duke, and I talked about HST Oil and Drilling Company and how Jack's death would affect the company. The Duke explained that when the company was formed, a clause in the contract that should one of the partners dies; the survivors would share his or her shares. To make sure that his wife and daughter were taken care of he sold them 25 percent of his shares to them. For the market value for which he paid our company now she gets her shear and his benefits. Upon his death Tyne Industries will be the majority stock holder.

The Duke told us we would be leaving the first thing in the morning pack your bags and leave them in the front hall that way we won't bother anyone when we leave. We will be going to Austin, Texas to file some contracts with the state at the capital office building. We will go back to the airport and fly to Washington D.C.

On the flight to Austin the Duke and Martin discussed the paper work he was going to file for Tyne Industries on behalf of Margret and himself to keep the company going when Jack dies and the legal results of his death. Margret will follow up the proper other paper work and Death certificate.

The Duke told her to keep him informed as to any problems with Jack's relatives, if any. The Duke told her not to say any thing to anyone about this. Or about his will or company business. If anyone wanted to know any thing about Jack's business they are to ask her lawyer.

Do not say any thing to Carol about this. Tell her that when we get back to England we want both Carol and Margret to come and stay with us for their visit. Thomas William and Martin will show them around Cambridge, London, and White Cliff.

The boys looked at each other smiled and said nothing. Martin had to keep him self from jumping up and down Thomas William laughed.

After the papers were filed in Austin, they returned to the airport and waited for the plane to Washington DC. I think Martin was getting use to flying he wasn't as nervous now.

After landing in Washington, we checked into the hotel relaxed and showered, the Duke told us to dress in our Blazers because we were going to the British Embassy to meet the Ambassador and his staff. Ambassador Robert Butler was a friend of his from Cambridge. Ambassador Butler was trying to get a meeting with President Truman. We won't know until we get there.

At the British Embassy, after meeting Ambassador Butler we posed for some pictures with his staff and the ambassador. The ambassador's secretary asked us to sign the Guest book and some pictures that the Duchess sent them of the Accolade Ceremony. Martin and I were surprised, we had not seen the pictures, and I asked the Duke if he had seen them, "he said no your Grandmother did things like that, told the photographer to send a set here. The Ambassador said that we could go to the White House to speak with President Truman. But we have to wait in the White House waiting room.

When we drove up to the White House Gate the guard asked us for some identification, we showed him our passports he called ahead to someone and told us where to drive to. When we got there and other guard stopped us and told us to leave the Limousine and go to the side entrance and would be met by one of the president's staff. Inside the entrance hall we were asked to show our identification. Now we had visitor tags and were told to follow the guide to the waiting room near the Oval Office. When we got there, there was a man waiting to see the president also the Duke introduced himself and the two of us the man said his name was Senator Lyndon Johnson. We exchanged greetings and the Duke told him we had flown in from Texas. That to our surprise, this was the begging of a long friendship for the Duke and the Senator, The Senator was from Texas. He and the Duke did all the talking after that. When the President's secretary came and got us, Senator Johnson said we must have some pull to get in before him and laughed.

After meeting the President and taking pictures we shook his hand and said good- by left the White House and drove down Pennsylvania Ave. We went back to the Hotel.

At the hotel The Duke called T.W.A. to book the next flight to New York City. We would be leaving at 3:00 P.M today. We packed our luggage and went down to the lobby to wait for the limousine to take us to the airport. At the airport in the waiting room the Duke told us we would be going to his office in New York City first to talk to his Lawyers and to give them copies of all the paper work he filed in Austin, Texas. Tell them about Jack Stewart.

Than go to New Canaan, CT. to pickup the rest of our clothes and say good-bye to everyone. "Martin I want you to call your mother in New Canaan and let her know we will be coming."

In New Canaan Mrs. Gibbons was making a big Dinner for us, The Duke was on the phone making our reservation for the flight to England.

After dinner the Duke told us we would be leaving in the morning. "Thomas William call your father and asks him to come over here so we could talk."

Thomas William called his father and asked him to come over as we will be leaving in the morning. The Duke wanted to talk to him about business and to say good-bye. When my father came over to see the Duke and say good-bye, he told the Duke that he would take us to the airport in the morning, than go to his office in Manhattan...

In the morning Mrs. Gibbons made breakfast after eating and thanking her we kissed her good-bye Martin said he would miss her, kissed and hugged her than said good-bye.

At the airport we checked in. than went into the waiting room. At the coffee shop that sold magazines, I went in with Martin while the Duke sat in the waiting room reading a paper he bough in the coffee shop. I bough a Life magazine a note pad and some pencils, Martin got a bottle of aspirins and two cups of tea and one coffee . After paying for the tea, coffee and magazines and other articles, we sat next to the Duke to wait. After a while a TWA stewardess came over to us and told us we were to board the plane she asked to see our passports and to give her the tickets. We did than she told us to follow her on board and showed us our first class seats. Than asked us if we wanted any thing to drink? I asked for a cup of coffee the Duke a tea and Martin a glass of water and a cup of tea. When the water came Martin took his aspirin settled back in his seat and buckled his seat belt and closed his eyes. The Duke took out his briefcase opened it and removed a ledger and some papers, and started to work. Not many passengers were on this plane it didn't take long to taxi out to the runway and do the pre-flight check and take off for England.

The Duke and Martin were not talking, the Duke working and Martin resting I was in the middle seat between them. I reading the Life magazine and thinking about the two separate businesses the Duke owned one in England and one in the United States. Both were Tyne Business but different names. I though of something to tie all of them together would be a logo to indentify them as one company under the logo. I pulled out the pad and pencils I bough at the airport in New York. I started to sketch a few ideas I had and came up with a sketch that I though would work well and needed to refine it. It took about two hours to make the sketch look good enough to show to the Duke and explain it to him.

The Duke looked over at me as I handed it to him and held my breath, and asked me to explain what it was. Now Martin was awake and listening to us, looking over to see the sketch.

I said that since Tyne Towers is the World Headquarters for both England and the United States, they have two different names in order to tie them together I thought the easiest way and cheapest would be to have the same logo for both businesses and any company after that, that you build or buy to use the logo saying "This is a Tyne owned company."

The Duke was surprised, and studied the logo and said he liked it and said "see what an education can do!" Than handed the logo to Martin and asked what he though of it? Martin said he thought it was magnificent and if the Duke liked he would research the logo to see if someone else was as smart as Thomas William. Than they all laughed. The Duke thought if an excellent idea. That started him thinking about what Thomas William had said about one company.

Than Thomas William said "if you notice the logo is an optical illusion. The large "T" in the center stands for Tyne, on the right the taller post is Tyne towers in England, and the left post is the United States across from the Tyne Tower. Now turn the logo upside down 180 degrees and you have an oil pump in Texas mounted on a "T".

Now what do both of you think about it? Martin was speechless the Duke "said this took a lot of brain power to think of something like this. How long have you been thinking about this?"

Thomas William said about 2 ½ hours. The Duke couldn't talk; he shook his head and looked at Martin. Martin was also shaking his head in disbelief. Martin said that if you could think up something as good as this in two and a half hours you're a genius. The Duke said that when they get to England he would do something about this; to Martin he said you and Thomas William go to the Cambridge Library and do the research on the logo. And to let him know what they find.

CHAPTER FOURTEEN

▼

Arriving back in London going through customs and having the Duke take a taxi to White Cliffs leaving Martin and I to take care of the luggage and get a limousine to White Cliffs was a surprise. We were tired and hungry the Duke said he would have every thing ready for us by the time we got to White Cliffs.

As promised the Duke had Matthew and the cooks ready for us as we pulled up to the mansion. Matthew carried the Dukes luggage inside Martin and I carried our own luggage in and lay on our beds in our rooms. The Duke had eaten and gone to his office in the Tyne Towers. Told Matthew to give us a message to call him after we had eaten, showered, and changed. We ate first called the Duke. He told us to take the Jaguar to the castle and than we would get our own cars and go to Cambridge. When we were finished with the library to call him and let him know what we found or did not find.

Martin and I cleaned up got dressed and took the Jaguar and drove up to the castle. When we got there Martin's father came to greet us told us that the Duke had called, that everything was ready for them and to rest up and go to Cambridge tomorrow morning.

We were tired that we went right to our rooms and went to sleep. In the morning Martin woke me up and told me to get ready for the big day at Cambridge, we had the cook make us breakfast and when we were ready to go. Martin's father had the Jaguar's washed and the tanks filled with gas. We thanked him, Martin hugged him and thanked him and said he would call him. We drove off.

Since we were still on summer break Martin said we can both stay at my apartment because he had packed a small bag and he had some school clothes at his place.

We rested and than went to the Cambridge Library. Checking the laws for company trade names, we checked on Copyright laws. Checking on logos and trade names that are registered with City of London. Nothing on any other trade name Tyne except Tyne Construction Company and Associates filed in the City of London.

Martin called the Duke to let him know that there was no other trade name Tyne. He would call us if he needed any more information.

We left the library, Martin said he was hungry and asked me if I had some money. I said "yes, I guess I was going to buy lunch." Martin smiled. We drove to London for lunch. I said maybe we should go to see the Duke and find out if he needs us for anything. I drove to Tyne Towers and parked in a reserved parking spot. Went into the lobby I went up to Alison the receptionist to get an ID badge for Martin and me. She smiled as I approached. I said two please. Alison laughed and "said with or without." I laughed and said you look familiar.

Alison "said that I know her sister Anna Gerail." I looked at her and "said I do?" I asked her "how do I know Anna?" Alison answered" you and Sir Martin took care of her at The Fairy Ring Campus she was a volunteer at the medical station.

I "said I would like to meet her again and talk to her and take her to dinner if she would like to go out with me. Would you tell her that for me?"

Alison said yes and she would give Anna Sir Thomas William's phone number. If he wanted her to have it. He handed her his card, the Duke had made for Martin and him. Sir Thomas William forgot about the badges and walked away. Sir Martin looked at him and smiled. Said "where are the ID badges?"He turned and looked at Alison who was waving the badges and smiling. Sir Thomas William walked back to Alison and thanked her, took the ID badges and turned and walked to the elevator and said nothing to Sir Martin. All the way up to the Duke's office Sir Thomas said nothing to Sir Martin who smiled all the way up.

When they got to the Dukes office Sir Martin asked Medford if the Duke was busy. Medford said he would check for them. Picked up the phone pushed a bottom and spoke to the Duke. Medford looked at the boys and told them to go right in.

The Duke was waiting for them he told them to sit down. The Duke said he received their message and thanked them for the information. He now has his Barrister working on the trade name, and Logo for Tyne Construction Co. Now they are to go back to Cambridge and get their clothes and move into White Cliff because tomorrow they are to start getting tutored by the teachers he has hired to help them with there studies for the next semester at Cambridge in September. White Cliff will be their class room for the next thirty five days. If they get good reports from their tutors he has a gift for them in August. Now go back to get your cloths and I'll see you at White Cliff, tonight for dinner.

Sir Thomas William asked the Duke if he would take a girl out to dinner he has not met yet, she was at the Fairy Ring Campus as a volunteer in the medical station. The Duke asked Sir Thomas William what her name is. He said Anna Gerail. The Duke smiled and said yes. Sir Martin smiled and looked at the Duke and the Duke winked at Sir Martin. The Duke "told them that he has instructed the Security office to have new permanent ID Badges for you and you will have your own parking space next to his. Oh and before I forget your new offices will be ready in about a week."

Sir Thomas William and Sir Martin went over to the Duke and both of them hugged him at the same time. The Duke smiled and said go pick up your new ID Badges.

They left the Dukes office in a daze and went down to the lobby to see Alison and get their new ID Badges. Alison had them ready.

Alison told Sir Thomas that she had called her sister and she said she would love to go to dinner with him and here is Anna's phone number to call her about the date. Sir Martin stepped next to Sir Thomas William and "asked Alison if she would like to make it a foursome for dinner" She "said yes." Sir Thomas William looked at Sir Martin and said "who invited you," Sir Martin said "someone has to keep and eye on you" than they all laughed everyone in the Lobby looked and smiled.

Sir Martin and Sir Thomas William went back to Cambridge to get their cloths and some of their books. Than drove to White Cliff to unpack and rested for a while. With nothing to do for the rest of the day, they decided to go shopping for some new clothes. But didn't know were to go. Sir Thomas William called Medford Walker the Dukes assistant and asks him if he would guide them to a clothing store in London. Medford gave them the name of the store that the Duke gets his cloths and where it was located and gave him the directions. Medford told Sir Thomas William that he would call the store and let them know that they were coming in. When you get to the store give them your names and every thing will be taken care of and have a nice day.

Getting to the store in the middle of London was no problem. Parking was a big problem. We parked in a pay to park garage. And went about two blocks to the Store. When we entered and realized it was a man's tailor shop. The name of the shop was Vincent Balducci's Men's Shop. In side to our surprise waiting for us was the Duke. No wonder Medford was helpful. The

Duke said he was here to help us with our wardrobe because if the Duchess was here she would be doing this for you. The manager came over to us and introduced himself to us he was Mr. Tayler Lord. And call him Tayler. He asked us to follow him. He led us to a large private dressing room with a lot of mirrors.

The Duke chose the style of suits, jackets, pants, and shirts. After and hour he said he had to go and we could pick out the rest of their cloths with the help of Tayler and his staff, and have a good time. The Duke turned to Tayler and told him to have any of the clothes that didn't need to be altered to send them to White Cliff and gave him the address, Tayler said he didn't need the address because everyone in London and maybe England knows were King George VI Knights live now. And are happy and proud to have them here. After the Duke left we picked out socks, underwear, asked one of the staff to pick out a dozen handkerchiefs for each of us. A few leather belts bring in some shoes for us to try on. After measuring for our foot size they came in with about two dozen boxes of shoes a dozen for each of us to try on. We picked out three pairs each. And told them that was enough for one day, asked if they would deliver the rest of the items. We asked Tayler to introduce us to the rest of his staff he wanted us to meet. They all came in to the dressing room a few at a time as Tayler introduced Sir Thomas William and Sir Martin to each of his employees, and some of there friends, we were happy to meet then all. After we said good-bye and left the shop I asked Sir Martin if he remembered where we parked the Jaguar. After finding the parking garage we drove to White Cliff.

Arriving at White Cliff I asked Sir Martin when he wanted to go out to dinner with the girls he said he had a better idea, why not come here for our first date. Than Sir Thomas William said way don't you call the Duke and ask him, it's your idea, he said OK he would pick up the phone and dialled the Dukes number. Medford answered and Sir Martin asked if the Duke was busy, if he was don't bother him I can wait until later to talk to him, Medford said he was never busy for you or Sir Thomas William and put Sir Martin through to the Duke. After talking to the Duke he turned to Sir Thomas and said," the Duke will be leaving for the castle Friday and spending the weekend there and thought that it was a great idea.

Sir Thomas William called Anna, Alison's sister to ask her the time she and her sister wanted to be picked up for Dinner. When Anna answered the phone Sir Thomas William "said he was sorry he did not remember her from the Fairy Ring Campus. And hoped she would forgive him."

Anna "said how could he remember there were only four hundred people there three hundred children and one hundred workers and volunteers any way it was a long time ago Anna said "I'm glad you called I need some information about the dinner. First when will we be going? Where will we be going, and important how shall we dress?"

Sir Thomas William said "Saturday night and we will pick you up about 6:30 P.M. Dress casual nothing fancy the place is going to be a surprise... he asked if there was any food she did not eat?" Anna "answered she like about any thing but did preferred sea food best of all."

Sir Thomas William "said that was great and was looking forward to seeing her Saturday and would call her Saturday to make sure nothing has changed. Now Sir Martin would speak Alison if she is there?"

Anna said hold on she would get her. Than he handed the phone to Sir Martin. After chatting with Alison for a while he said he would see her later tomorrow after they finish their studies with the tutor. Than she could give them the directions on how to get to their home. He said good bye and hung up.

The Duke arrived at White Cliff for dinner Thomas William waited for him to change and refresh and relax before he asked him for his suggestion about what they should have for dinner Saturday night. We are going to pick up at about 6:30 P.M. and bring them here but they think we are going to a restaurant. Thomas William told the Duke that he had asked them what food they liked they said sea food.

The Duke said he would talk Frederic the Chef and surprise all of you.

The Duke wanted to know how every thing went at Balducci's Shop today. Thomas William answered " after you left we didn't stay long," he told him what they picked out told them to deliver the clothes that didn't need altering. Mr.Balducci said he would deliver the altered cloths and make sure they fit and look good on them. The Duke smiled and said that's good.

CHAPTER FIFTEEN

▼

In the morning the tutors arrived at White Cliff. Matthew showed them in as we were having breakfast we asked Matthew to show them into the dinning room. When they came in we asked them to sit down and have some breakfast or something to drink. I introduced my self. And told them to call me Thomas William and this in Sir Martin, he laughed and said to call him Martin. And if anyone other than them is here please add the *sir* because the Duke is proper about that. Now what are your names?

My name is Fitzgerald Kent and this is Cecil Frost. Cecil said that he was Thomas William's tutor and to call him "C".

Fitzgerald said to call him Fitzgerald he was Martin's tutor, they wanted to thank the Duke for choosing them as tutors and are honored to be tutors for Thomas William and Martin. Martin said have a cup of tea and than we can get started.

Martin told them that he attends Trinity Hall at Cambridge is studying International Law. Thomas William attends Pembroke College at Cambridge his grandfather's alma mater, The Duke of Tyne's college. Thomas William said "I think it would be better if Martin and Fitzgerald went into the library and C and I stayed in the dinning room. They all agreed.

Thomas William went to find Matthew to tell him what they are going to do and would it be alright if they had lunch at 12:30. Matthew said he would take care of every thing and to study hard smiled and walked away. Thomas William liked Matthew a lot as did Martin in fact the whole family did.

This is the way we studied for the next thirty five days. The boys liked their tutors and got along fine with them. They worked hard to get good reports from the tutors and at the end they were rewarded with good grades from the tutors.

Saturday came and the boys went to pickup Alison and Anna at their home. They were invited in to meet their parents, Angelica and Andrew Gerail.

Mr. Gerail is an expert on shipping and ships for a large shipping company called World Wide Communications and Shipping. (WWCS)

Their parents were happy to meet us and thanked us for taking care of all the children at the Fairy Ring Campus and their daughter Anna. Anna is a beautiful blond, blue eyed girl about as tall as Sir Thomas William. The four of them left and Alison said she would call when they arrived at the restaurant the boys picked.

The limousine pulled in to the drive way of White Cliff the girls looked surprised and asked what the name of this restaurant? Sir Thomas William and Sir Martin laughed and said this is where we live, White Cliff. As they got out of the limo Matthew met them at the door and said "good evening", showed the girls to the parlor Sir Thomas William and Sir Martin followed them in.

After looking around the girls" said no wonder you didn't tell us the name of the restaurant are we going to dine here." Sir Martin said yes but we have no idea of what we will be having the Duke choose the Menu to surprise us all.

Matthew came in and asked if they would care for a glass of wine? The Duke chose a white mild French wine. They all said yes. As he went to get the wine Alison asked if she can use the phone to call he parents Sir Martin showed her where the phone was. Anna asked Sir Thomas William all about the Accolade and meeting the King and Queen. He answer that it was the same as when she met Princess Elisabeth at the Fairy Ring Campus. They were nice to him and Sir Martin that day. And he was to over joy to remember everything that happened that day. And still gets excited when he thinks of that day. Sir Thomas asked her what school she was going to and what was she studying?

Anna answered that she was taking a course to be a Dental Hygienist for her uncle who is a Dentist in Brighton. She is working at his office now as a receptionist.

When Alison and Sir Martin came back, Matthew came in with a tray and four glasses of wine, set the tray down on the small table, and went to get the bucket of ice and the rest of the wine. Matthew informed them that dinner would be served in a half an hour. He would call them when the chef told him it was ready. Turned and left.

Sir Martin and Alison were having a good time as was Sir Thomas William and Anna. Anna asked Sir Thomas William when his Birthday was.

He said March 9, and he is two months and two weeks younger then Anna. Anna was born December Twenty Sixth.

Matthew announced that dinner is being served. They all got up and went into the Dinning Room. There before them was a beautiful decorated table; with red and white roses along with gold candelabras, gold trimmed china and stemware everything was beautiful. The silverware was shinning. The lighting was turned down low. The atmosphere was fantastic. Alison and Anna were amazed everything was beautiful. Matthew indicated to the boys to hold the chair for the girls. As they held the chairs for the girls they saw the place cards with their names on them. Sir Thomas William and Sir Martin sat in their chairs.

Matthew rang for the waiter to start serving the meal. First they were served light crab bisque with a hint of Sherry. The next course was an Endive salad with creamy Tomatoe jelly.

The main course was Dover Sole stuffed with chopped spinach and mushrooms mixed with whipped cream flavored with brandy, the vegetable was a lightly baked tomato shell filled with succotash brushed with fresh creamy butter, Fresh baked hot rolls and bread. The wine served with dinner was Moselle.

For Dessert an Orange Charlotte served with Lady Fingers than Matthew came in with a standing ice bucket and a bottle of Champagne, popped the cork and served each of them put the Champagne in the ice bucket covered the bottle with a folded napkin and said to Sir Thomas William " if you need anything ring." Turned and left the dinning room. Sir Martin called after him and "said thank you for everything." Matthew smiled and closed the door.

When they were finished they all went out onto the enclosed terrace to look at the ships in the English Channel and listen to the waves roll onto the Dukes private beach. They all agreed that the meal and evening was more than any thing they had ever experienced. They talked all evening and at twelve o'clock they took the girls home and said they would call them tomorrow.

Sir Thomas William and Sir Martin received an invitation to Alison's Birthday Party on July 14 it will be a small family and a few close friends party. Sir Martin asked Sir Thomas William if he would be willing to share the expense and buy her a nice gift from Tiffany & Co. at Harrods on Kingsbridge in London. They choose a Cultured Pearl Necklace.

The day after Alison's party the Duke received a call from the Duchess that John Stewart died that morning. Margret, Jack's widow is going to have him cremated that was his wishes and since you seen he before he died. No need to come to Texas.

The Duchess said "after a small service, Margret and Carol will be leaving for New York with me and that we will be staying for a few days in New Canaan, CT. four of us will be returning to England. I will call you before we leave and let you know when we will be arriving in London." The Duke said hurry home because he missed her.

When he finished talking to the Duchess, he called his Barrister in London told him about Jack Stewart and to go ahead with all the necessary paper work to cover his business in the United States and to get in touch with his Lawyer in New York, if they needed any more information to get in touch with the Dukes office in London.

When the Duchess, Mrs. Gibbons, Margret, and Carol arrived at the London airport the Duke, Sir Thomas William, and Sir Martin were waiting for them as they came through customs. The Duke sent Sir Thomas William and Sir Martin to get the luggage. And they would wait for them at the curb to load the luggage.

Sir Martin drove the limo to White Cliff.

Matthew was waiting for them, asked the Duchess which guest bed rooms she wanted to use for her family. The Duchess said she trusted his choice and to let the boys know they will bring the luggage to the rooms.

The Duchess and Mrs. Gibbons went a bout getting lunch for everyone.

The Duke said he couldn't stay for lunch and had to get back to his office.

Kissed his wife, his Daughter, and Carol, and said he would see them at dinner.

Sir Martin was happy to see Carol again and told her. Carol said she was glad to see Sir Martin again and would he show her around London. He said yes.

The rest of the summer Carol and Sir Martin and sometimes Sir Thomas William and Anna would spend some time on the Dukes private beach at White Cliff.

Carol and her mother Margret are staying at the Tyne Castle with the Duchess. Sir Martin would pickup Carol and drive her to Cambridge to get her use to the campus and to show her around. When the time came for her to register and file all the necessary recorders for admittance, Sir Martin picked up Carol and her mother Margret to take them to Trinity Hall to show Mrs. Stewart the Campus Mrs. Stewart said that the Duke called her and told her he had found an apartment near the Trinity Hall campus for Carol and gave her the address for them to look at it and of they liked it they would call the landlord and make arrangements with him and get the keys. After registering they went to the address and found the apartment near Sir Martin's apartment. Carol loved the place and did her mother. Mrs. Stewart called the landlord and made all the arrangements and got the keys.

Carol said she needed some new cloths they drove to White Cliff and called the Duchess and asked her to join them at White Cliff and than go shopping for clothes in London, The Duchess said yes and to have Sir Thomas William to come and pick her up. Sir Thomas who was studying in the library said he would be glad to pick up his Grandmother.

At the end of August classes started for Carol and a week later for Sir Thomas William and Sir Martin and everything settled down to a normal pace.

The three of them were doing well at Cambridge with all their classes.

Margret called her father the Duke and asked him about selling her home in Texas and retuning to England to live. The Duke advised her to talk to her brother Wilfred and hear what he had to say before she made a decision about selling her home in Texas. About returning to England he said it was a great idea and would love to have her live at the castle with them.

There wasn't much dating going on between Sir Thomas William and Anna because Sir Thomas William was at Pembroke College Cambridge and Anna was in Brighton. Sir Martin saw Carol almost every weekend and would take her to the castle to see her mother and to get to know her grandmother, the Duchess. And Sir Martin can spend time with his family and go horse back riding with Carol, and some time with the Duke. They would show Carol the estate and what was left of the Fairy Ring Campus.

It was getting colder and closer to Christmas. The castle was busy with preparations for the Holiday festivity and the Duchess was busy with the decorations and sending greetings to everyone on her list. The Duke called Sir Thomas William and asked him to get Sir Martin and come to see him at his office at the Tyne Towers in London. Sir Thomas William picked up Sir Martin and they drove to The Dukes office. When thy got there he parked in his reserved parking space with his name on the parking sign the one next to his with Sir Martins name on it. They went into the lobby and saw Alison they went over to her she smiled and said hi here are your ID badges. Sir Thomas asked about Anna, how was she doing at Brighton? Alison said she was doing fine, Sir Thomas William asked Alison to give her a message for him; tell her he will call her but right now he is studying to get his finals in before Christmas break. They went up to the Dukes office Medford asked them to wait because he was on the phone with his Barrister they could go to see their new offices they are not ready yet. However they can take a look. As they went down the hall they were both excited about it now. As they first entered Sir Thomas William's office the floors were covered with paper to protect the carpet and the dust everywhere. The office looked beautiful to him than they went into Sir Martin's office it was in the same state as Sir Thomas William's. Medford called them and said the Duke was ready for them. They went into the Dukes office. The Duke told them to sit any where. He told them how proud he was of both of them and he received the report from the tutors and they passed with flying colors. Now for the good news your reward is: I am sending both of you to Windward Islands of Grenada, St. Vincent, and St. Lucia for two weeks of relaxation and sun. And make sure you come back with only a suntan if you know what I mean. Let me know when you can get away from college and I'll make the arrangements. Maybe at the Spring break. OK boys.

CHAPTER SIXTEEN

▼

After talking to her brother Wilfred, Margret Stewart made her decision to keep her residents in Texas by keeping her home and letting her brother Wilfred take care of it for her. She changed her will leaving every thing to her sole heir Carol and The Duke second in case any thing happened to Carol. This way everything will stay in the Tyne estate.

Christmas was a wonderful time for everyone the Duchess had invited everyone to the castle including all of her children and grandchildren to stay at the castle and if they needed any more room the Duke had the Fairy Ring Campus building renovated for the ones who wanted to stay there.

All new bath rooms' new windows and a new heating system and all new furniture the Duchess had chosen. Fresh new paint inside and out. The building looked beautiful everyone agreed the Duke and Duchess did a magnificent job on the old building. Now there was room for everyone in the family to stay at Tyne Castle for any event. Secretly the Duke was happy about the way things turned out.

A week before Christmas, some of the family members started to arrive first was of course was Margret, Than William Haven Heron, his wife Florence and their children; their adopted son Charles he took his step fathers last name, their birth children C.J. and Florence Ann Heron. Their second son Reginald Thomas Heron and his wife Ann Olympia arrived next.

And the last was Wilfred Mirgatroy Heron and his wife Irene Helen and their son Joseph Paul. The Duke and Duchess's Children used the same rooms they had when they lived there before the war. The grandchildren chose to stay at the new Fairy Ring Campus building.

The Duke had Mr. Gibbons clean and polish (with the help of Thomas William and Martin) the horse drawn carriage and the Wagon filled with hay for a hay ride around the estate in the snow. Everything was turning out perfect. They all had a great time getting to know each other.

On Christmas Eve the Duke and Duchess had a large dinner for everyone including all of their workers and live in help. Sir Thomas William and Sir Martin were most popular with the grandchildren and kept asking questions about the Knighthood and the King and Queen. Carol stood by Sir Martin and smiled. Sir Thomas William was with the Duke and Duchess Most of the time.

After dinner the Duchess had everyone go into the Library where the large Christmas tree was, logs burning and crackling in fire place, gifts for everyone some from their parents and others from the Duke and Duchess after singing some Christmas carols and wishing each other a Merry Christmas the Duke asked everyone to sit were they can find room as the Duchess with the help of her daughter Margret started to give out the gifts starting with the youngest grandchildren. Florence Heron, Christopher John Heron, and Charles Heron as the names are called he or she came up to the Duchess and hugged her and she kissed each of them. All of the children of the workers were called and given gifts. Than the Duke got up and said he and the Duchess want to wish everyone a Merry Christmas and he has some special gifts for the rest of his family. He went to the Christmas tree and pulled out a large red velvet bag trimmed in gold braid, he carried the bag to the Duchess. The Duke explained; he has two talented people on his staff at the Tyne Towers one is a relative and the other one maybe a relative. The first one designed a beautiful Logo for Tyne Industries World Wide and the other one did all the investigating to make sure no other company in the world can use this logo. Now what dose this have to do with Christmas? At that moment the Duchess handed the Duke a small ring box, no wrappings and will our Designer of the Logo Sir Thomas William please come and show your gift. Sir Thomas went to the Duchess and hugged her and she kissed him and whispered in his ear I Love You. The Duke gave him the box. Sir Thomas William opened it and stood for a long time before showing the ring the Duke had Tiffany & Co. make for him, and the rest of the jewelry. The ring was the Logo in White Gold with all diamonds it was absolutely beautiful he was shaking hard he almost dropped the box he handed the box to the Duchess and hugged the Duke and cried the Duke said that he worked hard for that gift. Now show it to everyone.

The Duke said here is the other half of the team Sir Martin as he approached he was nervous he hugged the Duchess and she kissed him the Duke handed him his box it was the same ring except for one small change, at each end of the top of the "T" was a beautiful red Ruby. He also hugged the Duke and said I Love You, with tears in his eyes. The Duke told everyone that he had rings for his sons with their birth stones in the center of the top of the "T". For his daughter she has a Brooch in the shape of the Logo with her birth stone in it. And for Joseph Paul he gets a ring also with his birth stone in the middle of the top of the "T" And for Carol she gets a brooch and her mother has something for her also, Margret handed her a small box with a ring like the others except it was White Gold and alternating red rubies and blue sapphires the ring was beautiful. The Duke called up all his workers and helpers, the house whole staff and each was given an envelope now everyone had a gift except two people The Duke and The Duchess but that didn't last long without knowing what was happing everyone ran a round the room and got a gift that they had hidden from the Duke and Duchess it was madding and a lot of fun everyone was laughing this was Margret and Carol's idea they all loved it and did the Duke and Duchess.

Mr. Gibbons asked if anyone wanted to go for a hay ride around the estate to dress warm he has a lot of new blankets that were in storage from the Fairy Ring Campus days. In the mean time Mrs. Gibbons and her staff are going to make Hot Chocolate for the children and Hot Spiced Rum for the grownups. And home made bisques and cake. For everyone.

Carol and Sir Martin went on the hay ride to give his father a helping hand and Carol to watch the children. They had a great time.

Sir Thomas William stayed with is parents to talk to them and let them know about school and the gift the Duke had given both Sir Martin and him for the good report they received from their tutors this past summer. They will be going to The Windward Islands, during spring break. The Duke opened two offices for Sir Martin and him in Tyne Towers in London. They have their own parking space too.

Thomas William said he can't believe the Duke did all this with the logo he designed. The ring is beautiful. Have you tried your ring on dad? Thomas William's father said yes and I have to admit I never thought you could do this kind of work. Thomas William "said neither did I? Let me know if you need a logo for your business and I'll see what I can come up with."

Church services are at 11:00 A.M. Christmas morning at the St. Andrews Parish Church who wanted to go be ready at 10:00 O'clock to make sure there is enough room in all the vehicles. When every seat in all the vehicles was occupied they were ready to go to church.

After the church service a buffet in the Dinning Hall for them the Duchess said not to eat too much because they were going to have a large Christmas feast starting at 7:00 P.M.

Sir Thomas William called Sir Martin and asked if they could talk and to meet him in the stable in about an hour. Thomas William was there and waited a few minutes for Martin. When he arrived he wanted to know what Thomas William wanted. Thomas William said "Martin we have been close friends for all my life, you are more than a friend you are my brother and I love you as my brother. I would want to know if you and my cousin Carol are serous or friends. I would enjoy seeing you two get married some day after you graduate. The Duke thinks you would make a great couple and welcome you as a grandson. If you and Carol go your seperate ways, I want you to know who ever you choose to marry is your business, remembered you will all ways be my best friend and brother. Martin was surprised and happy at what Thomas William said. Martin "answered that he and Carol care for each other. At this point in time, we have no plans about marriage. I like the idea, but not now. You said in three years it's possible until than we will keep seeing each other. Should anything change or when we make up our minds you will be the first to know. I love you for being honest with me and I'm being honest with you. We will keep this between us for now OK. They hugged and walked out of the stable together.

Two other people in the farthest stable which was Pembroke are Howard and the Duke. They look at each other and said nothing about what they heard nodded their heads. The Duke put his finger to his lips and pressed his lips closed, Mr. Gibbons nodded in agreement.

That conference between Thomas William and Martin answered a lot of questions that the Duke and Howard had about Martins education and Law degree. Now they both can enjoy the Holidays.

The Christmas Feast that night was a Glorious and magnificent affair. After two hours of eating and drinking, the Duke got up to toast his family and friends for all they did for him. Than he invited all of them to come to see the Tyne Towers and to let either him or Sir Thomas William or Sir Martin know when they wanted to go and they will make all arrangements. The Duke asked everyone to wear the gift he had given them to the feast, when the Duke sat down they all got up and showed their rings and brooches off and sang to the Duke and Duchess.

In the hills of Castle Tyne

There is a friend and a relative of mine

With humor and wisdom as everyone knows

We shall sing of his Wisdom that ever glow

He is generous and kind to all he knows

With love and friendship that ever grows

Lift your glasses on high and toast to The Duke of Tyne

For he is a good relative and friend of mine.

Sir Thomas William got up, "that song was written by two people who know him best, his wife The Duchess and his oldest son my father (he had a little help from his sister Margret.)"Everyone laughed and applauded.

CHAPTER SEVENTEEN

▼

Anna Gerail's Birthday was December 26th; Sir Thomas William sent her a dozen Red and White Roses and called to wish her a Happy Birthday. She was happy to hear from him and she thanked him for the beautiful Roses. Sir Thomas said that when his family leaves he would call her, and take her to dinner at a real restaurant, she laughed and said OK.

My Mother told me that the three of them, "your father, your brother and I would be leaving for the United States on the December 28th because he had some business to do for Margret and Carol about Jack Stewart's estate and that Reginald and his wife Ann would be leaving with them on the same flight. They will be going to see the Tyne Tower tomorrow and have dinner in London and stay at White Cliff over night and leave from there. The Duke has made all the arrangements."

Sir Thomas William said he would take the limo and drive them to London when they are ready to go to the airport, he would say good bye to then at the airport. They will be leaving on the first flight out in the morning.

Saying good bye wasn't easy for Sir Thomas William he had no idea when he would see them again, at his graduation in 2 years or maybe at a wedding in the family?

That night Sir Thomas William picked up Anna. He made reservations at a seafood restaurant the Duchess told him about. The restaurant was near the water front on the English Chanel near Dover. Making the reservation was easy because the owner knows his grandparents, The Duke and Duchess. The owner said everything will be taken care of, enjoy the food.

Sir Thomas William was wearing the Diamond Logo Ring when he picked her up. Sitting at the table in the Dover Restaurant, Anna "said is that a Christmas gift the Duke gave you, your wearing?" Sir Thomas William answered "yes and explained all about the ring. He told her that Sir Martin has one also his ring is a little different he has two rubies in his ring. The next time we go out with him I'll ask him to ware it.

Every family member went back to The United States except William Heron and his family they will be leaving after New Years.

Aunt Margret went back with her brother William Heron. Then to Texas to pack and send her personal items to England. Carol was at Trinity Hall.

Sir Thomas and Sir Martin made arrangements to welcome the New Year at the Duke and Duchess's Country Club. The Duke invited Anna's Parents Andrew and Angelica Gerail to join then. The New Years celebration was a great success and everyone had a great time. The Duke made a new friend in the shipping business.

Pembroke College has a new student in Sir Thomas William's classes his name is Abdul ibn Saud. Sir Thomas William and Abdul became fast friends because of their families and who they were. Auddy as Sir Thomas William called him; Abdul liked his new nick name because it didn't tell everyone who he was.

Auddy and Thomas William studied together with Christopher Smart who was a wiz at economics each one helped the other and all got excellent marks which in turn made their families happy. During study time in the library Chris asked Auddy and Thomas William where they were going for spring break. Sir Thomas William told them about the gift that he and Sir Martin received from The Duke and Duchess, a trip to The Windward Islands. Surprising Chris and Auddy by asking if they would like to join Sir Martin and him on the trip. They talked about it for a few days, made up their minds and said they would ask their parents if they could go. Each one came back with the same story. The Duke had to verify that they can go. When the Duke called Christopher Smarts father they agreed that Chris can go, the Duke assured Mr. Smart that there will be someone there to keep and eye on them at all times because of who they were. Than he called the King of Saudi Arabia and talked for a long time and agreed to all of the rules including Prince Abduls personal body guard. Now everything was set for the group to go. When the Duke called Sir Thomas William and told him it was ok to go and told him the rules they had to follow or else no one but Sir Martin and Sir Thomas William would go. When Chris and Auddy heard that all of them were going, they hooped and hollered and almost got thrown out of the library.

Sir Martin said that he was happy to have company on the trip and thought they were going to have a great time. The boys all agreed that they would be careful about not getting attention or notarity, for that would be bad for all of them.

The Boys returned from the Islands, sun tanned, smiling, and happy. And ready to finish the rest of the school year. Besides class work the boys talked about what to do this summer.

Sir Thomas William said he had to work at the Tyne Towers for his Grandfather but he can get time for a vacation if he wanted to. How would you two like to see my office at the Tyne Towers and go for lunch this week end?

Sir Thomas William said he had a better idea how about you guys spending the week end at White Cliff and going out to dinner. He said he would call his girlfriend Anna and see if she could get her sister and another girl to join us Saturday night for dinner how dose that sound. Chris and Auddy though that was a wonderful idea. Sir Thomas William called Anna when he had a break, at the Dentist's office. Anna said that was a great idea she would call Alison and her girlfriend Debbie and call him back later. He said no he would call her back when he was finished with his next class. Anna said that was a better idea and said good bye.

Sir Thomas William went to see Sir Martin to ask him if he would join Chris, Auddy, and him this weekend and take Carol to dinner along with Anna, Alison, and Debbie. He said yes, and called Carol who agreed to go and meet everyone. Everything was set to have a fun weekend.

Chris, Auddy, and Sir Thomas William left Pembroke Friday after their last Class. Sir Thomas William picked up Chris and his overnight bag first than Auddy and his bag. They took off for White Cliff. Getting there and meeting Matthew and the rest of the staff was part of Sir Thomas William's way of making everyone at ease and relaxed. Matthew was great at making people enjoy White Cliff. After getting Chris, Auddy, and Sir Thomas William settled in there rooms. They had a late lunch. Before lunch Sir Thomas William called the Duke and asked if he can bring Chris and Auddy into meet him at Tyne Towers the Duke said he would be happy to meet them.

Sir Thomas William parked in his reserved parking spot. Than went into the lobby. Alison greeted them and handed Sir Thomas William his ID badge. Alison smiled at Chris and Auddy and asked for there full names, Christopher Smart and will I see you tonight and tomorrow night also. Alison said maybe and handed him is badge. Than Auddy asked for a piece of paper and a pen, Alison looked at him and didn't say anything handed him a pad and pen. After writing his name and a note he handed the pad and pen back to Alison after reading the note she smiled and made his name badge "Auddy Saud." When he read it he thanked her. As they turned toward the elevator Alison said have a good day at Tyne Towers. When they got into the elevator Chris asked ", what did you write on the pad?"

You will have to ask her tonight. And laughed. At the entrance to the Dukes office Sir Thomas William introduced Medford to the boys and asked if the Duke was busy. Medford said" go right in," as they entered the Duke came around his desk and Sir Thomas William said this is My Grandfather the Duke of Tyne.

Auddy stepped forward and shook the Dukes hand and introduced him self, I am Prince Abdul ibn-Saud and happy to meet you. The Duke took his hand and smiled and said the pleasure his all mine. And thank you for coming. Than Chris did the same and introduced him self said I'm happy to meet you Sir Thomas William is always talking about you, now I see way, thank you for having us here. The Duke said anytime you are in London please come and see me. The Duke turned to Sir Thomas and said before you go please come back here and see me, all of you.

The boys went into the next office which was Sir Thomas William's it was now complete and beautiful. On the wall opposite from his glass desk was a large painting of The Duke And Duchess it was beautiful. Sir Thomas William said this is the first time I'm seeing the office completed and this painting of the Duke and my Grandmother I love them much. The two boys said they understand.

Than Sir Thomas William called Alison and asked her if she would send a security person up to give us a tour of the building. In about 5 minutes there was a knock on his office door Sir Thomas William said come in. The door opened and in walked Alison. She smiled and said you called for a tour guide here I am. They all laughed and said let's go. Alison knew everything about the building all the offices and the people who work here she said it was easy because she see's them five days a week. And knows their names, Alison is well suited for the job. And well liked by all of the people she introduced them to. At the end of the tour she took them back to the Dukes office and said good bye for now and left. When they entered the office, the Duke was standing in front of his desk with two gift wrapped boxes. He handed one to Christopher and one to Prince Abdul. Sir Thomas had an idea of what was in the boxes, when the boys opened their boxes they were surprised to find a gold watch with the Tyne Logo on the face of the Watch. They thanked the Duke and shook hands and keep looking at the watches. The Duke said look on the back of your watch, when they turned the watch over their names were engraved on the back and today's date. The boys thanked the Duke again. The Duke said wear them in good health. As they left the office they were trying to hold the empty box and put the new watches on, Sir Thomas William said give me the empty boxes and try the watches on.

Sir Martin and Carol came to White Cliff before 5:00 O'clock P.M. and relaxed, the five of them were in the observation deck on the upper deck. The Duke had it built for the Duchess and him to relax and look out over the English Channel.

Than it was time to shower and change and get ready to pick up the girls. Sir Thomas William asked the Duke if he can take the limo for the evening, he said yes. And have a good time.

First they picked up Anna and Alison went to Debbie's home and picked her up, than went to the Dukes Country Club for dinner. Sir Martin was there waiting for them in the dinning room, a three piece band playing when they got there. Sir Thomas William said he didn't know a band on Friday nights here; Sir Martin smiled and said the Duke had something to do with this.

About ten other couples were in the dinning room and more in the bar; they were all having a great time and danced all of the night. Alison and Chris where together all of the evening, Debbie and Auddy were the other couple no one knew about Auddy, this made him happy to be one of them.

At the end of June everyone was back in England. Sir Martin was being tutored for his Law degree and Carol and Aunt Margret were living in the Castle. Aunt Margret said that since the Duke got a tutor for Sir Martin she asked her daughter Carol if she would like to live in White Cliff and be tutored like Sir Martin. She said she would have to think about it for a few minutes than said yes. Margret called the Duke and asked him if he would give her the phone number of the company he used to get a tutor. The Duke gave her the phone number, she thanked him than called the number and asked Carol if she would talk to them about the courses they had to offer after talking to the representative she gave her the course she wanted to take and that she would be at White cliff with Sir Martin. Than handed the phone to her mother for the finances and who to make the check out to.

Driving down to White Cliff, Margret asked Carol if she wanted any money. Carol said yes and while there in London they can go shopping, when they arrived at White Cliff Sir Martin was there studying in the library Matthew knocked on the door and said Mrs. Margret Stewart and Miss Carol Stewart had arrived. Would you care to talk to them? Sir Martin said he would be right out after he finished his work he went into the dinning room and found them there. Carol said she would be staying here for a while to be tutored and than go to Trinity Hall to start classes in August. And get some extra credits for her degree. Sir Martin said that was a great idea. Carol said he mother would be returning to Tyne Castle after they go shopping. Mrs. Stewart asked where Sir Thomas William was. Sir Martin told her he went to see the Duke about going to Arabia I think that was what he said when he ran out and jumped into his car. Carol said he must be going to see his friend Auddy. Sir Martin said yes I think they are close friends now and I'm happy for them they are on the same level.

CHAPTER EIGHTEEN

▼

Auddy called Sir Thomas William at White Cliff and asked him if he would come and spend a couple of weeks in Dammam, Arabia with him at his father's palace on the Persian Gulf. They would go sailing on his father's yacht and swimming in the new pool at the palace. Sir Thomas William "said yes but needed to ask his Grandfather to make sure he can go." Give me your phone number and I'll call you right back as soon as I get in touch with him."

Thomas William called the Duke and asked if he can see him about a trip to Saudi Arabia. The Duke said ok. Sir Thomas William jumped in his Jaguar and drove to The Tyne Tower said hi to Alison got his badge and went to see the Duke. Medford waved him into the Dukes office. The Duke was on the phone as Sir Thomas William entered. He stood there and waited for the Duke to finish talking.

Duke hung-up the phone and looked at his grandson and "said that was the King Abdul of Saudi Arabia and we talked it over and made plans for you and I to travel to Arabia to see them. I'm going to do some business with the King. You and Prince Abdul will be on your own. I will be there for a day or two; I'll have to leave you to return on your own. I'm going to call the Airport and rent a plane to take us there. Sit tight until I make this call ok."

After talking to a pilot and making all the necessary arrangement. The Duke looked at Sir Thomas William and "said you did more in one call than I did in six months. If this deal goes through I'll buy you your own airplane."

Sir Thomas William was trying to make senses of all this, but gave up. Now we will be leaving tomorrow at nine o'clock in the morning, go pack and rest and I'll see you at dinner tonight.

When the Duke arrived at White Cliff for dinner, Carol, Sir Martin, and Sir Thomas William were waiting for him there was some small talk as they eat dinner but nothing else. Sir Thomas William was waiting for the Duke to say something about Arabia but nothing was said. Sir Thomas William didn't talk during dinner. When everyone finished eating the Duke said to Sir Thomas William he wanted to talk to him in the library. Carol and Sir Martin said they would be up in the observation deck.

The Duke and Sir Thomas William went into the library the Duke explained the phone call he had with the king this afternoon. The Duke said "Thomas William I have been trying to talk to King Abdul for about six months and what you did in one phone call is amazing. I have been trying to get the king to build a refinery in Dammam Arabia for a long time but he won't because he said unless I can show him that a refinery wouldn't interfere with the life of his people in Dammam he would not allow a refinery there. I asked the king if he would allow me to come and show him how it would benefit him and his people. The Duke told the king that because the Port of Dammam is the largest on the Persian Gulf and it's location to the Arabian Sea would insure that it would be safer than having only the one he has on the Red Sea, and if anything happened to that one he would have no refineries in his kingdom. If I built a refinery in Dammam he would keep refining oil and shipping it. Now he is thinking about it.

Thanks to you and Prince Abdul. I have my Engineers and legal staff standing by to make the deal.

Now I have to contact Mr. Gerail about forming a new company. We maybe go into the shipping business.

"If you do get the contract to build the refinery how long will it take?" Asked Sir Thomas William. The Duke "said about 2 to 3 years."

We will need soil samples to test, than we will need to build an off shore loading dock for the Oil Tankers and to bring in the materials to build the refinery and than put down miles of pipelines to the oil fields which shouldn't take long to lay pipes in the sand and bury them. Than we will need to build storage tanks for the refined oil to pump to the oil tankers in the Gulf. This of course depends on everything going right. With Luck when we are finished in three years everyone involved should be richer and happier. Now Sir Thomas William see what you did with one phone call.

The Duke smiled and said you have your work cut out for you and Sir Martin. There is one more thing and this is the most important thing no one is to know about this and I repeat no *one* this is important. Don't tell anyone in or out of the family Carol, Margret, Sir Martin, and especially your friends. I will tell who I think should know on a need to know basis and when they should know.

"I'm glad we had this talk because a lot of things went through my mind said Sir Thomas William, Now I know what to talk about and what not to talk about. I'm glad we are both on the same page in the same book. I'll tell everyone the truth that I'm going for a vacation and stay at my friends' castle in Arabia." The Duke did one of his knowing smiles. The Duke said tomorrow we will know where we stand with King Saud. The Duke asked Sir Martin to drive us to the Gatwick Airport which is off M 25 on the way to Brighton. The Duke told Sir Martin he would call him when he is ready to return to England in one or two days.

When we drove up to the private gate to the hanger area we saw a men waiting next to a De Havilland Dove Airplane, it was white with a blue strip across the length of the plane it was beautiful. Sir Martin pulled up to the man and the Duke asked if he was the pilot he said yes and you must be The Duke of Tyne. They got out of the Limo and shook hands; the pilot said his name was Frankie Laker. Sir Thomas William introduced himself and shook hands with the pilot.

He told the Duke and Sir Thomas William to call him Frankie all the people do. They climbed into the De Havilland Dove, Frankie asked Sir Thomas if he wanted to be his co-pilot and sit next to him? Sir Thomas William said yes. Got into the seat next to Frankie's seat and buckled his seat belt. The Duke climbed in the back and Frankie took care of the luggage. We got into the plane, buckled his seat belt and started the 380-horse power twin engines, did his prefight check list turned to the Duke and asked if he was all set to go? Than headed for the runway to wait for take off permission. Frankie handed me a set of ear phones to listen to the Tower and smiled when I put them on.

Sir Thomas William asked "Frankie how long is the flight to Arabia," Frankie said "since we will have head winds all the way it will take longer than usual." And there is 2 hour time change. They are two hours ahead of London.

The Duke sitting in the back behind the pilot took all this in and knew what he had to do.

I enjoyed the trip to Arabia. Frank (as I called him) and we became good friends. The Duke was busy with his paper work and making notes for his discussions with King Saud.

We landed at the private airport the king had built for him and his relatives to use, and invited guests. The King had a Limousine waiting for us when we arrived.

I thanked Frank for explaining everything to me about the airplane and how to navigate. Frank said "anytime you need to rent an airplane call me. The duke has my personal phone number. Have a good vacation and he winked at me and smiled."

The driver and his associate took our luggage and we got in the limo. When we arrived at the palace Abdul was there and waved to us as we got out of the limo. I went up to him and shook hands. Abdul said one of the king's men would take the Duke to see his father the king. Now follow me, your luggage will be delivered to your room. It wasn't a room it was a suite and lavish at that. Abdul sat in one of the biggest chairs I ever saw I started to unpack Abdul said he would have someone do that for me, now what would you care to eat? I said you choose and I'll wash up and change than we can eat and talk. When I went into the bathroom another surprise was there, a small marble pool with a fountain in the center in the middle of the room I guess that was the bathtub. When I changed and went back to the other room the food was there, now that's what I call room service. I asked Abdul not to call me Sir unless the Duke was around he under stood and said ok. Thomas William.

After we ate Abdul" said that we are go to the yacht it's my favorite place to be in this hot temperature, there is a breeze and we can walk around in our shorts or bathing suits. And maybe have some entertainment." Abdul asked "do you like blonds, brunettes, or redheads." Abdul had a smirk on his face which told me the whole story. I answered of the three or all of them." Abdul look surprised and" said you have done this before!!" Thomas William "said that when we get back to Cambridge I'll take you to a place that I think you will love going to ". Than said that this is going to be and out standing vacation.

After the Duke and King Saud signed the contracts on the second day, he came over to the yacht, and had a few drinks while King Saud had his personal plane gassed and ready to take the Duke back to England. We said goodbye and he left when the limo came for him.

Abdul and I sailed the Persian Gulf from one port to and other port around Saudi Arabia, first we stopped in Jubail the largest city in the north of Saudi Arabia than on to as RasTanura than into the Persian Gulf after a week and a half, I asked "Abdul what he though of the business that his father and my grandfather were doing, and dose he know anything about it, If I'm being to noisy tell me to shut up."

Abdul said "yes he knows something about what's going on but no details."

I "said the same here. Any way I have been having a wonderful time here with you and I love your country."

"I wish I can stay longer but my Grandfather has a tutor coming in for me I will get an early start on my studies and maybe get out of school early.

He wants me to graduate to learn the business that will be mine some day and become the next Duke of Tyne."

Abdul "said he sounds like the king saying the same thing."

"I will be leaving in two days I have to make arrangements to get to England. And would you drive me to the airport."

Abdul said "he would do better than that; he will ask his father if Thomas William can be flown in the Kings private plane to England. Don't worry about it."

After all arrangements were made and Thomas William was ready to leave, the two boys were not too happy but knew it would end soon, that they would see each other in a few weeks at Pembroke.

When School started in September everything settled down, Sir Thomas William, Abdul, and Chris were always together, studying or going out to dinner. Some times with the girls other times the three of them. After one of the early dinners with the three boys Sir Thomas William said" he had to make a phone call." When he came back he said" ok all set lets go."

Chris and Abdul looked at each other and asked where are we going? Smiling Sir Thomas William said "you'll see when we get there."

After about twenty minutes they drove up to a mansion. Than Sir Thomas William explained to the others; this is where you will have some fun that I will pay for as an introductory to this wonderful mansion. Follow my lead. Chris and Abdul followed Sir Thomas William. He knocked and the women who opened the door recognized him and told TWT to go into the sitting room and the girls will be down in a minute.

The women asked TWT to come to the desk on the far side of the room. They talked for a few minutes, than she picked up the phone and nodded to TWT, who went back to the boys and told them what to expect and make sure to use a condom, the girl will supply.

CHAPTER NINETEEN

▼

Every thing was happing fast this year, the Duke spent a lot of his time in Dammam, Arabia working with the king and his staff and the Dukes engineers trying to get every thing set and to build the refinery. Sir Martin, Carol Stewart, and I are in our last year at Cambridge. I'm still taking flying lessons from Frank and once in a while I go with him to Arabia to either pick up the Duke or drop him off. The Duke hired him as his personal pilot.

On one of his flights to Dammam the Duke asked Frank to look for an airplane that he thought that Sir Thomas William would like and was easy to pilot. He told Frank Laker he wanted to surprise Sir Thomas William. The two of them settled on an American Piper Vagabond. White with a blue strip running the length of the plane, his name painted on the pilot side in Dark Blue; Sir Thomas William Heron. Frank took care of everything and had the plane assembled in the airport he uses for his plane. When the Duke heard he pays rent to keep his plane there the Duke bought Frank Laker a piece of land near Great Yarmouth, England to build an airport with a hanger and control tower. It was a gift to Frank Laker. Needless to say Frank was over joyed at having his own airport and named it The Laker Heron Airport. This made the Duke happy and proud.

Before my twentieth Birthday the Duke said "that he had to go to Dammam Arabia, asked "would like to join him," not giving it a second thought I said "yes."

Than he asked me to call Frank Laker and make arrangements for the trip, than let him knows what time the flight leaves. I called Frank and explained the situation and we needed a flight time for tomorrow. Frank said he had to check out something and would call me right back. I gave him my phone number and said I'd wait. After a half an hour he called back and said the flight leaves at 5:00 P.M. because of a sand storm in Arabia and they would have to wait for it to clear before they can land. Sir Thomas William said all right I'll call the Duke and tell him. Sir Thomas William called the Duke back and told him about the sand storm. The Duke said ok mumbled something and hung up.

I packed a small carry on bag. The next day the Duke called and said he had to take some maps for his engineers and would pick him up in his limousines.

When we arrived at the airport there was no plane or Frank. The Duke said you better go to the hanger and find out if there is a problem.

Sir Thomas William went to the hanger and opens the door, the hanger was dark and he called out to Frank. Than all the lights went on and a crowd of people yelled Happy Birthday, and sang Happy Birthday to you to me.

I couldn't speak; I stood there not believing what was happening. I don't remember who was there. They all were smiling and clapping, they started to sperate into two groups one on the right and one on the left, which lead to a pathway to a white airplane with a blue strip running along the length of the plane. It was a new model Piper Vagabond an American made light, easy to pilot plane, it was beautiful as I got closer to the Vagabond I saw my name on the pilot side of the plane. The whole thing was a live dream. Than the Duke And Duchess wheeled out a large Birthday cake in Blue and White with twenty burning candles.

It was an amazing day.

Than Frank came over to me and said you have to watch out for those sand storms. Than it hit me they had this whole thing planed for a long time.

I was happy I'll never forget it. Sir Martin, Carol, Anna, Alison, Abdul, Chris, and even Matthew and Medford was there and smiling. I had to thank everyone I claimed up on the box that part of the plane came in and thanked everyone.

Than the Duke invited everyone to White Cliff, for food and drinks, come on over and enjoy.

It was a wonderful day to remember and enjoy over and over again. I had to talk to Frank Laker about the Vagabond and asked when can I pilot it? He said in about three weeks and in the mean time you can go for your pilot's license. I think you're ready. I'll make an appointment for you.

A week later I had my license but had to wait to make sure the new Vagabond was safe and had to pass inspection.

I finished College in April with above average marks and would graduate in June with the rest of the school.

The Duke said he was going to have a big graduation party at the castle for the three of us Carol Stewart, Sir Martin, and Sir Thomas William, we can invite we wanted to and they can stay at the Fairy Ring Lodge as it was now called by you guessed it the Duchess. All of the staff at White Cliff and Tyne Tower will also be invited It is an exciting time of my life. I can't wait to start working at Tyne Towers with Sir Martin and Carol Stewart.

I moved from my apartment at Pembroke to White Cliff at the end of April. And started working at Tyne Towers for my grandfather.

At first he said I had to learn all about his business in England, than the United States. It's more complicated because he had his own business and was in partnership with others in the United States.

I started on the business in England which took me about a week and a half. I wrote down all the questions I had and went to talk to the Duke about them. He answered all my questions than I went back to my office and started on the United States.

I was surprised to learn that the Duke owned 75% interest in HST Oil Company and Margret and Carol owned 25%. My father sold his shares to the Duke. He wanted to start a new company with his brothers William and Reginald. They formed a new company WRW, William, Reginald, and Wilfred. An import and export business dealing mostly with foreign made automobiles. The majority British and Italian makes.

Sir Martin and Carol were getting serious and some whispers about marriage had been mentioned, but no one asked them about the rumors. They were still in college. Sir Martin was now the Tyne Construction Co. International Lawyer.

Carol and her mother Margret are planning to open an American Fashion Dress Shop. High end. The Shop will be next to Vincent Balducci's Men's Shop. They are going to specialize in New York and western style clothes for young adults. Also shoes and bags will be available.

We graduated and had a fantastic party at the castle, it lasted two days. A few days later I called Abdul and asked if he wanted to have some company for a few days I'll ask Christopher if he wanted to come along. We need to relax and spend some time with you because we won't be seeing you that much any more. Abdul said come on down he would love to have us.

I called Chris and told him what I had in mind; I asked if he was interested in coming with me.

He said "I'm not doing anything I may as well go." We made plans that I would pick him up and drive to Frank's airport where my plane is kept.

After taking off and heading for Dammam, Arabia, Chris and I talked about what he wanted to do or has he got a job. Chris said he needs to do some training in a real work environment to get some experience. I asked if he would care to work at Tyne Towers with me as an advisor to me on all finances and learn the business from the ground up. Because the Dukes Company is now world wide and we can learn together. If I wasn't at the controls of the plane he would have hugged me. Chris said "I would love to be your adviser when do I start?" I said "you already did, you are my advisor and co-pilot and you're going to take flying lessons from Frank when we get back from Dammam, you will share my office until yours is ready.

When I landed in Dammam at the king's private airport Abdul met us with a big smile and wave. Chris couldn't wait to tell Abdul about his new job.

The three of us had a great week and Sir Thomas William asked Prince Abdul to keep in touch and come and stay with them at White Cliff. Abdul said he would.

Than they got into the newly gassed Vagabond and took off .Chris said he felt sad about leaving Abdul he's a real nice person. Sir Thomas William agreed.

Chris said that Abdul told him that he was happy that we will be working together at the Dukes Company.

Chris and I worked well together he has a great sense of humor and can be serious when it came to finances.

At a meeting in August, with the Duke, Sir Martin, and I and the head of the finance department for Tyne Construction Co. Christopher made a suggestion about the way the finances were recorded. He said they should be a follow up check on all records by an independent Dept. and any errors found will go back to the records dept. to be verified.

The Duke called a meeting of all department heads and told them that he is creating a new department to be called Financial Quality Control. The person in charge of that dept. will be Mr. Christopher Smart, who will answer to me.

I was happy for Chris. He was surprised and happy. The Duke told him he would have to hire his own people to do the job and he will need a personal secretary of his choosing both he and I knew who he would ask first. After the meeting he went down to the lobby and called Alison aside and asked her if she would care to be his secretary. Alison said yes, but she would have to get a replacement for her job. After she said yes he told he about the new Department he will be heading.

Things were working out for Tyne Construction Co. I had to go to the United States on some business and to check on HST Oil Co. in Houston, Texas, and than meet with my brother Joseph Paul in Los Angles he wanted me to meet some of his clients.

I asked the Duke if I can take Christopher Smart with me and introduce him to the people in our Tyne Industries Companies. The Duke thought that was a wonderful idea.

When we landed in New York we took the limo to New Canaan, Connecticut to visit my mother and father we stayed over night at their house and left the next morning for our office in New York. I introduced Christopher Smart to everyone and let him explain the new procedure to them; they were impressed and happy to see me again. I thanked them all for having us here and now we have to go the airport and get on a plane for Texas. We landed in Houston, Texas and got a limo to our downtown office building and introduced Christopher Smart to everyone and again let Chris explains the new procedure to them. As in New York they were impressed and willing to go along with the new setup.

We stayed over night in Houston near the airport, had a great steak dinner and went to our rooms and sleep for about eight hours. In the morning we showered and changed cloths packed and went to have breakfast Chris had something he never had before for breakfast, Steak, eggs, and grits, he loved it. I had ham and eggs no grits, and coffee. Chris had tea. Than we went to the airport for our plane to Los Angles. When we arrived in Los Angles we went to my brother's office. He was expecting us; I had called before we left Houston. I introduced Christopher Smart to Joseph Paul; they took to each other like a duck to water. They liked each other. Joseph Paul said he couldn't wait to show us off to his clients he said we will be staying at his house in Long Beach which is not to far. Here is the address everything is ready for you there. I'll call you later and until than go and relax and sit on the beach or watch from my deck, you will love the view.

CHAPTER TWENTY

▼

When we got to Joseph Paul's house, I was surprised; I guess I shouldn't have been after all we were in an America. His house was something else you can see the décor told you he was a bachelor all the furnishings were all male. We unpacked and showed and sat on the deck and watched the beautiful scenery and the Pacific Ocean too. The Girls where parading up and down the beach. Their swim suits where not getting wet.

When Joseph Paul came home we were on the deck half awake and half watching the parading females all shapes and sizes.

Joseph Paul said wake up, we are going shopping for some clothes for the two of you because we are invited to a party tonight.

Joseph Paul drove us to Los Angeles to the men's shop where he gets his clothes; he introduced us to the owner Mr. Andrea Palladio. Joseph Paul told Mr. Palladio what he wanted for us, he than took us into a private dressing room and we tried on a lot of clothes the Duchess wouldn't have chosen for us. I told Chris not to worry about the bill it will be charged to Tyne Industries on my expense account. Joseph Paul told Mr. Palladio that we would be back in two hours to pick up the clothes, than I gave Mr. Palladio all the information on the payment of all the clothes. I gave him my father's name and phone number. Mr. Palladio said that isn't necessary, he knows him well and ware the cloths in good health.

Than we went to have something to eat at one of the restaurants Joseph Paul goes to all the time. After a slow luncheon we had, we returned to Mr. Palladio's for our clothes. And thanked him for everything and said good bye.

Than we went back to Joseph Paul's to rest and get ready to go partying.

A lot of people and movie stars who Joseph Paul introduced us to; one in particular was Baron Francis Brooke and his Daughter MaryAnn Brooke.

When Joseph Paul introduced Baron Brooke to me his daughter MaryAnn got excited and said she has heard much about Sir Thomas William and the Fairy Ring Campus and was glad to meeting him. We had to come all this way to America to meet you.

I asked MaryAnn where they lived. She "said in Coventry, England."

I asked what you are doing in Los Angles. MaryAnn answered "we are visiting my mother's sister who is married to and actor in Hollywood." Would you care to meet them?"

"I said yes," MaryAnn took my hand and lead me to group of people and introduced me to her mother Mrs. Mary Brooke and her aunt Mrs. Elsa Leighton. And her husband Mr. Leighton the actor and a funny man, we talked for a long time about England and the king and queen. MaryAnn and I walked away to look for Joseph Paul and Chris. When we found them it was late I asked MaryAnn when she was going back to Coventry, she said in about week. I asked her for her phone number in England because we would be leavening the day after tomorrow, for New York and than back to England. Tomorrow my brother had made plans for us to go to Hollywood. And see how movies are made. MaryAnn said you will enjoy it; she was there a couple of times with him Aunt Elsa.

After visiting Hollywood the next day and seeing all the stars, we had lunch and than went to Joseph Paul's house because we had to get up early to get to the air port in Los Angeles for our flight to New York. Were we will be waiting for our connecting flight to England?

The next morning Joseph Paul took us to the Los Angeles Airport and said good bye. We waited for about an hour and a half, and boarded the plane for New York. We landed early because of heavy tail winds we had longer to wait for our flight to England.

While we waited in the New York airport Chris and I talked about the trip I asked him to write up a report on the Tyne Industries we visited and give us his ideas on the good things and the bad things at each place we visited. He took out his leather folder that had a pad and pencil from his carryon bag. And started to write the report, by the time our flight was called he had two pages of remarks, I was glad the Duke hired him; he will go far in this business.

We landed at the London airport and took a limo to White Cliff were Chris got his car and said see you tomorrow at Tyne Towers. I carried my luggage which was much bigger now thanks to my brother. I asked Matthew where was everyone, he "said at the opera, it's a big night for the Duke and

Duchess. They donated money to keep the opera open. They said they would be late don't wait up for them." I asked Matthew to wake me up about 6:30 I wanted to get to the office early, Thank you.

In the morning Matthew had the cook make breakfast for me and after I got showered and dressed in my new clothes I went down to eat, I thanked Matthew for wakening me and having the cook make breakfast, he smiled and "said he loved wakening up the cook. It made his day watching the cook mutter to her self all day." I said with a smile "you're a cad," and left.

At the office, I was writing my report on our trip to the Tyne Industries in the United States when Chris knocked and came in, he "said good morning."

I told him his new office was ready there are a few odds and ends to finish. Alison may move in today if she would care to Chris's office was next to Sir Martin's office than next to Chris's office was a conference room and continuing down the hall there are more offices. The entire assistant's offices were across from the person they worked for. On the same side was a mail room, an office supply room and of course a tea room (coffee room for Sir Thomas William). Every office had a window view of London.

Sir Thomas William did not have an assistant; this up set the Duke because Medford had to do some of Sir Thomas William's work also.

The Duke told Sir Thomas William he had to get an assistant as soon as possible.

Sir Martin hired a court secretary he met at Cambridge. He was studying law but had to drop out it was too much for him but he loved the law. His name is Alfred Newman.

Sir Thomas William had an idea he would try to get an assistant at Cambridge. He called Vice Chancellor Richard and asked to meet him, the Vice Chancellor told him he can come at 10:00A.M. Because he would be free than.

After talking to Vice Chancellor Richard in his office he made a few phone calls. When finished talking to his niece, I had a new assistant. Her name is Isabella MaryAnn Rita Beveridge she is the Vice Chancellor's niece. Isabella was one of the children who were at the Fairy Ring Campus. She was twelve years old when she first came to The Fairy Ring Campus.

Isabella graduated from a school in Spain where her mother is from. Isabella is a beautiful looking woman, specks' Spanish fluently.

I told the Duke about Isabella he "said Sir Thomas William you never cease to amaze me.

The Christmas of 1949 was a big event for everyone. We were having the ritual Christmas Eve Feast for the family at the Castle as usual the Duchess did a beautiful job with the Holiday Décor inside and out this pleased the Duke.

Everyone of the relatives who could be here came, my mother and father, brother Joseph Paul of course Aunt Margret and Carol Stewart, Reginald and his wife Ann, William and his family, Sir Martin and his mother and father and brother and sister. I invited Isabella and her family, Christopher Smart and his family (mother and father) I also invited Abdul, but he thanked me but said his father is having a problems with his younger brother Abdul Al Saud he would not be here. I went to the Duke and told him about what Abdul told me he said he knew about it and there is no interference with the refinery or any other projects that the Duke is working on. The Duke asked Sir Thomas William should he hear any thing about Saudi Arabia to let him know immediately.

The rest of the Christmas Eve event was all joy and happiness everyone who was there got a gift from the Duke and Duchess. I of course was surprised again by the Duke and Duchess they gave me a Rolls Royce from the Duke and a chaffer from the Duchess. The Duchess "said I will meet the new chaffer tomorrow when he comes here with the Rolls Royce."

And to top the evening off Carol showed off her new engagement ring. It was beautiful and a large diamond. Sir Martin stood there and smiled, we can see that they were happy and in love. My aunt Margret couldn't be happier about the engagement. I went over to Sir Martin and hugged him and congratulated him at that point we know our two lives will change from now on. And I was happy for him and he knew I was. They have set the date for June of 1950, next year. Sir Martin asked me to be his Best Man I said a happy yes.

The Duke made the annual announcement about going to church on Christmas Morning. The services Start at 11:00 A.M. everyone going to church must be ready and in the cars by 10:30 A.M. than off to St. Andrews Parish Church. And God Bless everyone you too Tiny Tim.

After church everyone had a hearty brunch. Than off to the hay rides with Sir Thomas William in one horse drawn wagon and Sir Martin in the other. Making snowballs and snowmen singing carols and laughing all the way.

The evening feast was catered that way the employees can enjoy the feast and dress up. Than the Duke and Duchess gave out the Christmas envelopes and bonuses, to his employees, Merry Christmas to one and all said the Duke and Duchess.

The New Year 1950 looked promising for the Tyne Companies and for the Tyne family.

CHAPTER TWENTY ONE

▼

Sir Martin and Carol are house hunting in and around London. The Duke told them he was in the process of building a luxury apartment building in Eastbourne on the English Channel east of Brighton, if they would wait until the end of this year the building should be ready to move in, in the mean time after you are married you can live at the Tyne Castle or White Cliff.

After talking it over they decided to live at White Cliff until the apartment is ready which would be six months. Because they both worked in London they would be closer to their jobs. Margret Carol's mother was happy for them.

Sir Thomas William and Christopher Smart were working on a system to streamline the accounting system to incorporate the entire Tyne Company business world wide. They asked Sir Martin to join them and give them some advice on international laws on trade.

Christopher Smart passed his flying test and received his license to pilot a small plane. Now he and Sir Thomas William can share piloting the Vagabond that the Duke And Duchess gave to Sir Thomas for his birthday.

The refinery was almost finished and ready to start testing along with the loading docks for the ships to load with the oil from the refinery. Sir Thomas William and Christopher Smart would fly to Saudi Arabia to check on the work in process and to see Abdul and stay for a day or two to be with him. Sir Thomas William would always bring the Duchess a lot of Dates and figs he would buy at the markets in Dammam. The Duchess loved dates and figs and have the cook at White Cliff make desserts for the Duke and the rest of the family. And take some back to the castle.

When Sir Thomas William and Christopher Smart returned to England they reported to the Duke on the progress of the work that was completed and what had to be finished. The one thing left was to test the ships at the docks to make sure every thing was set for each tanker to dock empty than fill to capacity with ocean water than steam out to the Arabian Sea and pump out the water than flush the tanks with a mixture of bleach and water to make sure the tanker can move out of the port of Dammam Arabia and into the Arabian Sea. Now the shipping company G&H Shipping can start bringing in the empty tankers and anchor in the Arabian Sea. G&H Shipping is a company that Mr. Andrew Gerail and the Duke formed and is partners with a third person Sir Thomas William Heron KGM.

The Duke and Duchess decided to change a few things to make it easier for Sir Thomas William to take over all of the business owned by them that when the time came for him to take over the leadership of the Tyne Companies there would be no problems.

The preparation for the wedding for Sir Martin and Carol was getting everything organized. Carol and her mother Margret picked the date of June 23, 1950. Than what church or place where the wedding take place? That will be St. Andrews Parish Church. Where Pastor Richard Flaws is a friend of both families and he will marry them.

Carol and Isabella, (Sir Thomas William's Personal Assistant) became good friends. Carol said that Isabella is a beautiful person; Carol will ask her to be her maid of honor.

Who and how many bridesmaids will she have? Than where will the reception take place and how many invited guests will be there be? And who will they be?

Than she wanted a Paris designer named Chanel to design her wedding dress. And Carol will design the rest of the dresses, her Maid of Honor and the bridesmaids.

Margret Stewart and Carol picked out the wedding the invitations that would be printed. The guest list had to be approved by Sir Martin and his parents.

Sir Martin had to pick his groomsmen and talk to Carol about the formal or informal tuxedos for the men?

Sir Martin and his best man Sir Thomas William will wear the same outfits they wore to the Knighting Ceremony by King George VI.

The major portion of the arrangements for the June wedding is well under way.

Carol has chosen her new girl friends for her bride's maids Isabella her maid of honor, Sir Thomas William will be her partner, Sir Martin's Sister

Erica and her partner, Prince Abdul, and Debbie Lloyd (Carol's room mate at Trinity Hall) and her partner Christopher Smart.

The Duchess was asked; to arrange the reception at Tyne Castle. This will include the food and flowers. The Duke asked the Duchess if she and Margret would like to have tents set up for out door entertainment, music and dancing. A food and bar tent can also be set up. Sir Martin and Carol told them it was a great idea bit of Texas in England. The wedding took over all the conversation for the next few months.

In April the King of Saudi Arabia and the Duke arranged to have a Grand Opening of the new Arabian Oil Refinery and shipping port in the Persian Gulf. We were all invited to Saudi Arabia and to stay for all the festivities that was to last for a week. The Duke closed the office for that week and who worked on the project was also invited, the rest of the people had a week's vacation.

Prince Abdul and Sir Thomas William arranged to have a bachelor party for Sir Martin on the king's yacht. The King, the Duke, Sir Thomas William, Prince Abdul, and Christopher and a few of Abdul's brothers were there. No alcohol but plenty of other drinks was available and a lot of food and a lot of dancing girls that no one was to touch. All in all it was a nice party.

After the Grand Opening on the third day, the Duke and Duchess and Mr. and Mrs. Andrew Gerail and a few others left for home. The rest of us stayed and sat around Prince Abdul's pool and did absolutely nothing. Friday Frank Laker came to take us all back in a rented 12 passenger De Havilland 114 Heron. Chris and I had the same thought about the 114 Heron it was beautiful. I can picture our logo and the sides of the plane. Chris and I will have to talk to The Duke about this.

Returning to England meant that Sir Martin and Carol's wedding will be here before you know it. The Duke had given them a wedding gift. Their honeymoon will be paid for by him and the Duchess any where they wanted to go. And that will be kept a secret.

As the wedding grew closer Carol and Sir Martin had all the bridal party at White Cliff each weekend for a get together. Sir Thomas and Isabella were getting friendly as was Christopher and Debbie. Abdul couldn't be there every weekend Erica had to call Abdul and tell him what was happening with the Wedding party. Sir Thomas William was surprised when Erica told him the Abdul got his license to pilot a small airplane.

On June 1, 1950 everything was ready for the wedding. The Duke and Sir Thomas William had a surprise for everyone at the reception. The Duke and Sir Thomas William were the only ones who knew about it, it would happen at night during the entertainment.

Every thing was set for the big day. The families where staying at the castle. All of the out of town guests were also here. They were also staying at the castle or The Fairy Ring Lodge.

Sir Martin, Sir Thomas William, Joseph Paul, Prince Abdul, and Christopher Smart where all staying at White Cliff.

Carol and her mother Margaret were at the Castle and over seeing the arrangements for the wedding and the church rehearsal and the small party after the rehearsal at St. Andrews. All the Groomsmen and Sir Martin came during the day with their luggage.

After the church rehearsal and since it was a beautiful night Sir Martin said that the tents were up we may as well use them and who wanted to can go out and sit under the tents, it was great idea. Sir Martin asked the Duchess if she had any large candles, The Duchess said yes and to ask your father to show you where they were. Sir Martin asked his groomsmen to come with him and get the candles and put them on each table and light them Everyone enjoyed the soft glow of the candles and the drinks and small talk with there friends and relatives. It was a wonderful evening.

The morning of the wedding day the weather was warm and sunny. You couldn't ask for a better day for a wedding. A beehive of activity as soon as everyone had breakfast and all the cars were being lined up and ready to take them to church and back. Six limousines: were standing by.

The first one was for the Duke And Duchess and Mr. And Mrs. Gibbons.

The second was for Margaret and Wilfred and his wife Irene (Sir Thomas William's Mother and Father) and Joseph Paul.

The third was for Reginald and his wife Ann. William and his wife Florence and their children.

The forth was for Mr. Gibbons' brother and his wife and Mrs. Gibbons' sister and brother.

The fifth was for the groom Sir Martin and his Groomsmen.

The sixth was for the Bride and her Bridesmaids.

By the time the bride's limo got to the church all the people were in side and waiting for the ceremony to begin.

Sir Martin, Sir Thomas William was in the front of the church by the side entrance waiting for the music to start. Sir Thomas had the wedding rings in his vest pocket.

The rest of the groomsmen where waiting at the top of the Church steps for the bridesmaids.

The Bride and maid of honor got out of the limo. Carol looked ravishingly beautiful. Isabella the Maid of honor helped her with her wedding gown as Carol walked up to the top of the church steps. After getting adjusted and took a deep breath and nodded to the sexton indicating she was ready the organist started to play and everyone in the church was standing.

As first couple Christopher and Debbie started down the aisle Debbie looked beautiful in her light pastel green gown. The three bridesmaids wore white broad brimmed organdy and silk trimmed hats. Debbie carried a nose-gay of white roses

The second couple was Abdul and Erica her gown was a pale pink in the same style as Debbie's she also carried a nose-gay of white roses.

After making sure that Carol was ready and extending her bridal six yard long train. Isabella in her light purple gown and white organdy hat looked beautiful. Isabella carried a light purple orchid nose-gay. Isabella started to walk down the aisle.

As the music intensified, Carol in her floor length wedding dress of White Organdy with a white silk over lay and organdy trimmed white silk train started to walk down the aisle, on her beautiful long black hair she wore a silver crown studded with white pearls (her mother had given to her). The crown was attached to a short silk veil to cover her face. She carried a nose-gay of white orchids and white roses. Carol was a beautiful bride.

The Duke was standing next to her she took his arm as they walked down the aisle toward the waiting groom. When they reached Sir Martin the Duke gently lifted her veil, kissed her and took her hand and stepped aside and gave her hand to Sir Martin Gibbons KGM. Than turned and sat next to the beautiful and smiling Duchess. Pastor Richard Flaws started to perform the wedding ceremony. In 45 minutes Pastor Flaws announced they were husband and wife and presented Sir Martin Gibbons and Lady Carol Gibbons to all present. The smiling couple descended the alter steps as the triumphal music played and clapped as they exited the church. It was a beautiful wedding.

And now on to the celebration, the Tyne Castle and the Tents were all decorated with white and pastel colors of ribbons that were waving in the breeze. The Duchess did a superior job on all the décor both inside the castle and the outside in the tents.

When everyone from the church including Pastor Flaws had arrived. The food and drinks were ready. A line for tea and coffee. Everyone started to clap for the Bride and Groom to Kiss and pose for pictures. Everyone was having a good time than the band arrived and started to play soft music. As the celebration continued into the late afternoon the Duke asked all the guests to go into the castle and relax, the waiter had to setup and arranges the tables and chairs for the wedding dinner and dancing the portable dance floor the Duke had built for this wedding. When everything was setup and ready Sir Thomas William asked the guests to return to the out side, there is tables with their names on each dinner setting find your table and keep standing until the bridal party is ready to enter. When everyone was ready the band played a John Philip Sousa March and the Bridal party was announced as they entered and stood by their table until the Bride and Groom entered than Sir Thomas William asked the waiters to serve the champagne toast. Sir Thomas William asked all the guests to raise their glasses of champagne. He made his toast to the Bride and Groom:

"I grew up with him and loved Sir Martin all my life and since the Duke, Sir Martin and I went to Texas and my first meeting with Lady Carol. I knew this day would come. Sir Martin was in love with her the first time he saw her, she kissed me because I'm her cousin) and smiled at Sir Martin. He was in love. All I can say is to have lots of babies and lots of happiness and lots of health. And long and happy marriages as my Grandparents the Duke and Duchess.

The band played a Blue Danube Waltz for the Bride and Groom than asked the rest of the bridal party to join in. Than we all sat, eat and drank. We were all having a good time when the Duke called me aside and said "now ". I went to the band asked all the guests to go to the front of the tent and told the guest the Duke and I had a surprise for the bride and groom I told the band to play Tchaikovsky 1812 Overture (that was the signal for the Fireworks to start).

A lot of oohs and aahs and clapping and yelling.

All the Guests and the bridal party were having a wonderful time and it was the best wedding they ever attended. Sir Martin came over to me and handed me a small box with a note attached, it read "I will always need you as my best friend I didn't need to open the box because I had given the box to Sir Martin a number of years ago.

The End

Author Bio

While in the United States Navy for eight years, I had a great opportunity to travel. Crossing the Atlantic Ocean six times. Sailing around the Mediterranean Sea, Going to countries Spain, Italy, Greece, Turkey, Algeria, and France. In Cannes, France, I met an actress named Grace Kelly. She told me she was making a movie in Cannes and Nice. Passing through the Panama Canal, sailing on the Pacific Ocean up the west coast of the United States to Seattle, Washington and back down to San Diego, California.

Why would I write a novel about England? Because My grandfather loved telling me stories about England and the royals (as he called the royal family) His home town London, traveling all over England for work, finding none unmarried he sailed to the United States and becoming a master carpenter. His stories fired my imagination for years. This novel is about one of my fantasies